What people ar

Hope for Allis continues the story of the McRuer family in southwestern Manitoba in the 1890s. Patricia Linson's richly detailed, semi-fictional account portrays the joys and hardships of these hardy pioneers. Her story is presented through the eyes of thirteen-year-old Allister "Allis" McRuer, picking up the story from the preceding volume where his long-cherished hope of attending school nears fruition. It is a story that will be enjoyed by readers young and old, and especially those interested in Manitoba history and the challenges of turning the wild Canadian prairies into an agricultural breadbasket. Highly recommended.

—Gordon Goldsborough, PhD
head researcher and webmaster for Manitoba Historical Society.
Author of *With One Voice: A History of Municipal Governance in Manitoba* (2008); *Delta: A Prairie Marsh and Its People* (2015); and *Abandoned Manitoba* (2016)

Hope for Allis is Book Two of the Allister of Turtle Mountain series. The McRuer family has donated land for a one-room school house, and Allister is eager to complete Grades Seven and Eight. The new teacher is very harsh but responds to coaching from Allister's mother. Allister's father feels that farming takes priority over education, and his older brothers are establishing homesteads. His twin does not share Allister's desire to focus on his studies. The reader is immersed in the life of Scottish settlers in southwestern Manitoba in the 1890s—a skittish horse and frightening buggy ride, learning to swim and fish, surviving blizzards, and a "new-fangled" idea to keep a water pump flowing in the dead of winter. We share Allister's joys, concerns, and desire to contribute to his community in a different way.

Modern readers will be reminded that school was once a luxury and encouraged to be grateful for the opportunities they have now. I've really enjoyed Books One and Two and am looking forward to Book Three—*Becoming Bob*.

—Karen Mason, physician (retired)

Whether you remember pioneer times personally or taste that life for the first time as you read this book, you will enjoy delving into the historical lives of these real people! Enter into their joys, sorrows, frustrations, and victories!

—Helen McCormack
educator, freelance writer,
contributor of devotionals for twenty years to *The Minot Daily News*
contributor of devotionals to *Today is the First Day*
and contributor to the blog for the *MissionNext* website

Move over, Ms. Wilder ...

Rich in descriptive language and engaging writing, once again Patricia Linson adeptly takes us back to the wonders of 1890s Canadian pioneer life. In *Hope for Allis*, the second book of the Allister of Turtle Mountain series, we follow young Allister's journey from his first day of school in 1893 to the days following his graduation from the eighth grade. Readers are transported to 1890s Manitoba as they experience Allister's joys, tribulations, and quest for a fulfilling future.

Hope for Allis is a terrific addition to any school, classroom, or guided reading library—providing a wonderful opportunity for students to compare life today to that of long ago. A must read for all, but especially for fans of historical text such as *Little House on the Prairie*.

—Judie Anderson Offerdahl
elementary teacher, poet, freelance writer
author of "Chinese New Year," *Highlights* (February, 2018)

Readers will care about Allister and feel his determination and frustration in his pursuit to achieve a better education than the rest of his family because he knows farming is not his passion. His faith and trust in God grows to help him overcome the obstacles he encounters. Patricia carefully scatters Bible scripture and prayer into the text of her engaging storytelling. The Allister of Turtle Mountain series could be in the collection of a middle grade parochial school library.

—Sue Kohls Shetka
freelance writer
author of the action rhyme/poem, "It's Me!" *Highlights High Five* (2008)
the poem, "Our New Baby," *Highlights Hello* (2014)
and the poem/song, "Rock-a-Bye, Darling," *Highlights Hello* (2015)

Allister of Turtle Mountain Series - Book 2

Hope for Allis

P Linson

2023

Patricia E. Linson

HOPE FOR ALLIS
Copyright © 2018 by Patricia E. Linson

Cover illustrator: Patricia E. Linson

Scripture are taken from the Holy Bible, King James Version, which is in the public domain.

Printed in Canada

ISBN: 978-1-4866-1636-7

Word Alive Press
119 De Baets Street, Winnipeg, MB R2J 3R9
www.wordalivepress.ca

MIX
Paper from
responsible sources
FSC® C016245

WORD ALIVE
—PRESS—

FSC
www.fsc.org

Cataloguing in Publication may be obtained through Library and Archives Canada

In loving memory of Robert Allister McRuer, my grandfather, who financially supported my undergraduate education.

Contents

Book II: August, 1893–July, 1895

Acknowledgements

With gratitude, I remember my grandfather, Robert A. McRuer, his daughter, Reta McRuer (deceased), and my father, Harry Titcombe, for their anecdotal information about the life of my main character, Allister.

I am grateful for my husband, Irv, who gave me access to a 1969 reprint of the 1902 edition of the Sears, Roebuck and Co. catalogue. In addition, Irv helped with the editing process of the manuscript of *Hope for Allis*.

I appreciate my friend, Donna Larson, for cleaning my house while I wrote the original draft of this book.

I wish to thank Michele Scott, head librarian of the Boissevain and Morton Regional Library, for providing a photo of the stone schoolhouse built in Boissevain, Manitoba, in the 1890s.

My hat is off to the research librarians of the Ridgedale Library, Minnetonka, Minnesota, for helping me locate information about Native Americans of North America, and specifically First Nations' legends about twins.

I appreciate the 2008 summer staff of the John E. Robbins Library at the University of Brandon, Brandon, Manitoba, for keeping the library open long enough for me to access information about Manitoba's 1890s school curriculum and eighth grade exam content.

I thank the members of the writers' critique group in Shoreview, Minnesota, for their suggestions for this book.

I am grateful to Laurie Toth, my art class instructor, for her guidance in perspective, methods, and materials during my creation of the cover illustrations for *Book I: A Boy Called Allis* and *Book II: Hope for Allis*. Laurie passed away unexpectedly two weeks after I turned in the cover illustration for *Book II* to Word Alive Press. I will greatly miss her ready laughter and keen eye.

I appreciate Sylvia St.Cyr of Word Alive Press, and Kerry Wilson, editor, for their assistance in the publication of *Hope for Allis*.

chapter one

Miserable Morning

Manitoba, August, 1893

*O*h boy! *The first day in our new school!* Allister thought. He turned over and nudged his twin brother awake.

"The rooster hasn't even crowed yet," Jim grumbled. "Why so early?"

"We've got barn chores to do before breakfast," Allister said. "You do remember school starts today, don't you?"

"Oh, alright." Jim sighed and rolled out of bed.

Allister led Jim in a race through their chores before they returned to the house to gobble the breakfast that Mary, their older sister, set on the table for them.

"Slow down, you two," Mother said. "School starts at nine o'clock. It's only eight."

"I know, but Jim and I want to get there early today."

Mother handed each boy a brand new scribbler and pencil. "Come straight home at noon for dinner. Mary and I'll have it ready for you, even if Father and your brothers haven't come in yet."

Allister and Jim kissed Mother on her cheek, hugged their little sister, Jessie, and ran out the door. After bolting across a pasture and climbing over a wooden fence, the twins were panting by the time they reached the schoolyard that occupied the northwest corner of their father's homestead. Allister checked the school. It was locked. Jim checked the stable. "No one yet," he said.

It wasn't long before they saw other children running or riding across prairie fields. Behind one group of children walked a tall, thin, young man.

"Here comes the teacher," Allister said, who had met him before.

The teacher walked up to the schoolhouse door. Turning around on the front step, he addressed the children in the schoolyard. "Good morning, children. I'm Mr. Webster, your teacher. In a few minutes, it'll be time to start school. When it is, I'll come out and ring the bell. Now you can play."

The children stood awkwardly about the schoolyard, not knowing what to do. Some knew each other. Others didn't. A little shy, some stood together with their brothers and sisters. One taller girl stood alone, quietly watching everyone. Allister counted fifteen boys and girls.

"Hey, Charlie," Jim hollered, "let's play tag." Running over to one of the younger boys, he touched him and ran away, hollering, "Tag, you're it!"

That broke the ice. Soon everyone was running and laughing or hollering.

Clang, clang, clang. The teacher stood next to the open door, ringing the bell. Running past him, the children noisily filled seats, sitting next to siblings as they would have in church. The teacher marched to the front of the room and turned to face the children with his arms folded across his chest. "What are you, a herd of cattle?" he shouted. "Quiet!"

Fifteen mouths fell silent and sixteen heads dropped. Allister frowned. *When my family came from Quebec, there was no school near our homestead. After waiting over a year to finish the sixth grade, I was hoping for a better start to our first day,* he thought.

"Everyone go back outside." The teacher swept a long, bony finger towards the open doorway, his lips tight.

Trooping outside, the children stood in a cluster near the door, unhappily staring at their teacher. Allister stood with his hands stuffed in his pants' pockets. *This is terrible. Most of these children have never been to school before. How are they supposed to know what to do when the teacher hasn't said what he expects of us?* Allister said to himself.

"Line up. Girls in one line. Boys in another," the teacher ordered, glaring at everybody. He crossed his arms over his chest and waited, impatiently tapping one foot. "Now, girls, go sit on the right side of the room."

When all the girls had entered, he said, "Boys, sit on the left."

After everyone was seated, the teacher stood at the board and wrote his name. "My name is Mr. Webster." Pointing at one of the girls, he asked, "What's my name?"

"Mr. Webster."

"No!" he shouted. "Stand up when I call on you, and then answer the question!"

Turning pink, the girl stood and repeated his name.

Erasing his name, the teacher, pointing at Jim, ordered, "You there, come to the board and write my name one letter at a time while Allister spells it."

Jim came to the board while Allister stood and spelled, "W-e-b-s-t-e-r."

After Jim returned to his seat, the teacher asked, "Who knows the name of this school?"

One of the boys popped up and said, "I do, sir. Wood Lake School."

"Correct. Now write it on the board."

"Umm ... sorry, sir. I can't."

"Alright then ... you," the teacher demanded, holding out a piece of chalk and pointing at the tall girl. "What's your name?"

The girl stood. "Mabel, sir," she said, before taking the chalk from the teacher. Printing carefully, she wrote WOOD LAKE SCHOOL across the top of the blackboard.

"That's correct," the teacher said when she finished. "I want everyone to write their names on the board, one at a time. Since you're already at the board, Mabel, you start."

During this exercise, Mr. Webster discovered that he had two Teenas, two Johns, two Georges, and three James in the class. He also learned that five of his pupils couldn't write their names, so he did it for them.

Opening a notebook on his desk, the teacher asked how many years of schooling each student had and wrote that in his book.

We have one eighth, two sixth, one fourth, and twelve first graders. Most of the first graders are much older than six, Allister thought. *Umph! I'm glad I'm not Mr. Webster.*

"Everyone stand up," Mr. Webster directed. "Jim, come hold the Union Jack. Now let's sing 'God Save Our Queen!'"

Although Mr. Webster blew a note on a small pitch pipe and started the song, few sang. The teacher wrote the words to the song on the board, saying, "Maybe this'll help you remember."

Most of these children have never been to school before. How could they have learned it? Allister thought. *Most can't read it, either.*

The teacher tried to lead the song again, but the second time was no better than the first. Mr. Webster gave up.

Sitting at his desk, Mr. Webster flipped through some pages in three books. "Let's start the day's lessons with some arithmetic," he said, rising and handing a book to Mabel, another to Jim, and a third to Amy. "Take out your pencils and copy these problems onto the first blank page in your scribbler. Do them while I work with the rest of the children."

Jim pushed the book into the middle of the desk he shared with Allister. Without speaking, the twins settled into the task of copying the problems. But when he had finished, Jim shook his head and whispered, "I don't remember how. Do you?"

Nodding, Allister demonstrated how to do the first one. Smiling, Jim whispered, "Now I remember. We did this kind of problem in our sixth grade class. They're easy."

Not many minutes into the arithmetic period, Allister heard sniffles coming from Amy. He looked at the teacher. *Surely Mr. Webster can hear her.* But the teacher stayed focused on the first graders who were sitting on the recitation bench and learning to count. When Mr. Webster also ignored Allister's raised hand, he left his seat without permission. Leaning over her desk, he whispered, "What's the matter?"

"I don't know how to do this," she sobbed, pointing at the problems in the book.

"Copy the problems into your scribbler and then come sit in front of Jim and me," Allister said. "We'll help you."

Before he returned to his seat, Allister located a piece of chalk and a slate. When Amy moved to the seat in front of them, he gave her the slate and chalk. "Copy the first problem onto the slate," he whispered.

She followed his instructions, and then he said, "When you work this kind of subtraction problem, remember to borrow across the zero like this."

After watching him work the sample problem, Amy managed to work several of her problems on the slate with the twins' help. When she could do several on her own correctly, she returned to her seat with her scribbler.

A short time later, Teenie approached Amy and broke the quiet in the room by saying loudly, "I have to go!" The room filled with snickers. Amy looked at Mr. Webster, but when he didn't even look up, she took her little sister by the hand to the outhouse.

Before anyone had finished their lesson, Mr. Webster shouted, "Recess!"

The class dropped their pencils and chalk and ran out the door like an overeager cattle herd. There was pushing and shoving at the girls' outhouse until Jim hollered, "Hey, stop that!"

"Take turns," Mabel shouted. "Line up!"

Over at the pump near the schoolhouse, one child pushed the handle while some of the others cupped their hands to catch the water for a drink.

"Does anyone know how to play Red Rover?" Jim asked.

"I do," Mabel said.

The children collected around the tall girl as she explained how to play the game.

"We're first," James shouted, after he and Jim had chosen their teams. "Red Rover, Red Rover, send Emily right over."

Since she was the smallest girl, Emily couldn't run hard and fast enough to break through the line of children holding hands. Pouting, she held hands with members of her new team. Taking turns, the captains called until Jim's team consisted of only him and Allister.

Mr. Webster appeared at the door just then and rang the bell. Standing directly in front of the door this time, he waited for his students to line up. When they had, he said, "Boys first." Trooping in, the boys and then the girls continued their playground chatter.

"Quiet!" Mr. Webster hollered when he got to his desk. "Get back to work."

In a few minutes, Mr. Webster came over to check on the twins' work.

"Sir, this was easy," Allister complained. "Could we try something harder?"

Looking a bit flustered, the teacher strode over to the bookshelf. After selecting another book, Mr. Webster flipped pages as he walked back across the room. "Try this," he said, without explanation.

Allister stared at the page of math problems his teacher had set in front of him. *He's the teacher. Shouldn't he make sure Jim and I know how to do this?*

The teacher started across the room.

"Mr. Webster, sir."

"Yes, Allister?"

"I think the problems you gave Amy were a little too hard for her. Jim and I tried to help."

"Good. I'll check on her later," the teacher said. "While I check Mabel's work, Allister, would you take a few minutes to help Teenie and John with their addition? Jim, help the first graders write their numbers."

A few minutes later, Mr. Webster moved from Mabel's desk to Amy's. Then Mabel got up to help some of the beginners too.

Allister looked over John's shoulder first. Somehow 26 + 14 didn't add up to 310. When Allister checked Teenie's scribbler, she was making the same kinds of mistakes. *They have no idea how to do this*, Allister thought. *Should I suggest easier work for them?*

Before Allister could decide what to do, Mr. Webster told everyone to put their arithmetic away. The teacher erased the board and wrote the word "Elocution" and a silly sentence below it. "Amy, please read this sentence out loud."

She stood and read, "See saw seasells by the seasore."

"No, not correct. Mabel, you try. Go slowly ..."

She stood and read, "She ... saw ... seashells ... by the ... seashore."

"Correct!" the teacher said, "Let's try all together now."

Pointing word by word, Mr. Webster read and everybody repeated. The faster he went, the more everyone's tongue got tangled. More students laughed than repeated. "Stop!" he yelled.

Erasing the board yet again, Mr. Webster wrote out the patriotic song, "God Save the Queen." Pointing word by word, the teacher read and the students repeated. After he had gone over the song twice, he erased it. "Georgie, tell me the whole song."

Georgie, the littlest boy, stood with his knees shaking. After stammering through the first line, he stopped, hung his head, and said, "Can't remember anymore."

Mr. Webster slapped his desk with his ruler, causing everybody to jump. "See that strap hanging on the wall?" he shouted. "I'll use it tomorrow on anyone who can't remember. Georgie, you can't remember because you weren't paying attention!"

Georgie's older brother, Charlie, raised his hand. "Please, sir, let me try."

Mr. Webster stood next to his desk with his arms folded across his chest, frowning; then, after letting out a sigh, he nodded. Charlie stood and made it almost all the way through the lines before he faltered. Some whispered, coaching from behind him, and helped him finish successfully.

"Finally!" the teacher exclaimed, looking at the clock. "Noon break. One hour!"

The teacher reached into his desk and pulled out his dinner pail. Turning his back to the children, he started eating before anybody had moved.

Remembering his mother's instructions, Allister left for home immediately. As he and Jim climbed over the fence to cut across the pasture, Allister saw the older children exit the school with their younger siblings to sit outside in the grass together and eat food cold from their dinner pails.

chapter two
One-Room School Days

"**M**other, our first morning of school was terrible," Allister complained as his mother dished up her famous creamy tomato soup and sliced some fresh-baked bread.

"Boy, was it ever!" Jim agreed. "Mr. Webster yelled at us and called us a bunch of animals ..."

"No, he didn't." Allister plopped his spoon into his bowl of soup and frowned at his brother. "Don't exaggerate, Jim. Tell Mother the truth."

"Well, alright. Mr. Webster called us a herd of cattle. And he slapped a ruler on his desk in a temper. Got mad at us for doing things that he hadn't even told us we weren't to do. He hasn't strapped anybody yet, but he's threatened to do that tomorrow—to even the littlest boy, if he can't remember the words to a song."

Mother sat and listened, not saying a thing.

"The arithmetic he gave us was too easy, and the work he gave to Amy, Teenie, and John was too hard," Allister said. "He seems to expect everybody to do arithmetic problems without showing us how to do them."

"Boys," Mother said through firm lips and with a stern look, "Father and I expect you two to obey the teacher, even if you disagree with him or his methods. Maybe this is his first teaching job. Don't fuss. Give him time. This was only the first morning. I'm sure things will get better."

When the twins started for the back door at 12:40, she warned, "Come straight home after school. I need your help to harvest the garden. Then you have barn chores before supper, because you'll probably have homework afterward."

The afternoon didn't go any better. For the reading lesson that day, Mr. Webster gave Teenie, John, Amy, Jim, Allister, and Mabel readers and told them to read their assigned pages silently. The teacher also put a dictionary on the desk between the twins with instructions to share it with Mabel.

"How do you use it?" Jim whispered, looking doubtfully at the huge volume.

"Not sure," Allister whispered back. "I've always asked Mother or Mary when I didn't know what a word meant. Guess we'll have to figure it out ourselves."

Mr. Webster called the names of the first graders with no schooling to the recitation bench. Out of the corner of his eye, Allister saw the teacher point at an alphabet chart. Repeating the names of the letters, he tried to get the ten beginners sitting in front of him to learn all twenty-six letters in one lesson. Soon Allister saw beads of sweat lining the teacher's forehead.

Without asking permission, Allister got up to sit next to Amy to see how she was doing. For the next ten minutes, he helped her sound out new words and explained a few to her. When the teacher sent the beginners to their seats to practice writing their A, B, C's, Allister sat between Charlie and Georgie with a slate to demonstrate the letter A. Charlie had no trouble copying the shape, but Georgie's first As looked more like Hs. Allister showed Georgie how to make an A again and again. The results were the same.

Remembering that his mother used three dots in the form of a triangle to help his sister, Jessie, draw the diagonal lines of that letter, Allister drew three dots on both his and Georgie's slates. "Now connect the dots like this," Allister instructed as he demonstrated on his own slate. This time, success! Allister beamed at his littlest pupil. "Excellent, Georgie! What a beautiful A. Want to try again?" Georgie grinned and nodded and waited for Allister to draw the dots again. In no time, the little boy could space the dots correctly and draw the connecting lines on his own.

While Charlie and Georgie practiced the letter B, Allister looked around the room. Jim and Mabel were helping the other beginners draw their letters. The two first graders with several months of schooling were sitting on the recitation bench, stumbling through the short sentences in their readers. Exhibiting great impatience with each student's poor reading, Mr. Webster began shouting, "No, no! It's not that. Can't you see?" It wasn't long before he abandoned the torturous reading exercise. Abruptly, he called, "Recess!"

Dropping their books promptly, everybody ran outside. James started another game of tag, with the water pump as the "free zone."

After recess, Mr. Webster tried a different subject. Opening a book on his desk, he read several pages aloud. "Alright, children, who was the first King of England?"

Jim looked at Allister, and Allister looked at Mabel.

"Excuse me, sir?" Charlie asked.

"Yes, Charlie?"

The boy stood and asked, "What's England?"

Mr. Webster slammed his book shut. Walking over to a map hanging on the wall near the left corner of the room, he pointed with his ruler. "This country here."

"Excuse me, sir?" Georgie said, raising his hand.

"Yes, Georgie?"

Georgie walked over to stand next to Mr. Webster in front of the map. "Why does the paper have so many colours on it? Is it a picture? Doesn't look like anything I've ever seen. Not a barn. Not even a tree. What is it?"

The teacher clapped both of his hands on the top of his head. Allister heard him groan and mutter something about having a very long way to go. "Never mind," Mr. Webster said and sent Georgie back to his seat.

"Let's try some dictation." The teacher handed out chalk and slates to everyone. "I say something, and you repeat it and then write it."

But this exercise was also a disaster. Mr. Webster dictated too much too fast for the students to even repeat correctly, let alone write. When the selected students wrote the dictated letters or sentences on the chalkboard incorrectly, the teacher tightened his lips and slapped the ruler against the top of his desk. "No, no, no!" he hollered.

Allister shook his head. *How is this fair? Most of my schoolmates have never written anything in their life before today.*

Taking the chalk from the students, the teacher erased their attempts and wrote the correct letters or sentences himself. Mr. Webster continued this frustrating experience for twenty minutes. Then without ceremony, he announced, "Three o'clock. School dismissed. See you at nine o'clock tomorrow."

Dropping everything else, the children picked up their dinner pails and scrambled out the schoolhouse door. Turning back before he exited, Allister looked at the room he had helped to put in order a month ago. He saw mud from the schoolyard under every seat; chalk and slates on the floor; pencils, scribblers, and books scattered across desks; and a chalkboard full of writing. But there was no time to help tidy the room. Remembering his mother's instructions and gripping his scribbler, he raced across the pasture after his brother.

Minutes later, as he and Jim changed into their work clothes, Allister watched his father and older brothers through a bedroom window. They were returning to the barnyard with the two-wheeled cart and the wagon piled high with the farm's second crop of hay. Allister breathed a sigh of relief. Thankfully, being in school all day had helped him avoid one of his least favourite jobs—haying.

An hour later, while he was carrying a sack of freshly-dug potatoes from Mother's garden, Allister watched Mr. Webster leave the schoolhouse. Turning down the road heading west, the young man walked with shoulders slumped and his head down. He had one hand stuffed in a pocket, while the other held onto the strap from which his dinner pail hung over his shoulder and thumped against his back with each trudging step.

He needs some help, Allister worried. *But who can help him, and how?*

That evening after supper, Allister opened his scribbler to work on the math problems he had copied from the second assignment.

"What are you doing?" Jim asked before he looked at Allister's work. "Oh!"

"Forget yours?"

"Uh-huh."

"Don't worry. Help you tomorrow after I get some help from Mother tonight."

When Mother sat down to help Allister, they did more than homework. They talked at length about Allister's day at school.

The next day during morning recess, Allister asked Jim and Mabel over to the paddock fence to talk. Two horses joined the children at the railing to beg for handouts.

"We three have the most schooling," he said. "Let's give our teacher as much help as we can."

"Alright," Mabel agreed, stroking the neck of the horse she had ridden to school. "But how are we going to finish our own work? I hear I have to pass an eighth grade exam before I can graduate."

So that's why she didn't offer to help Amy yesterday or today, Allister thought. Out loud he said, "If we take turns helping the other students and do some of our assignments at home, we can finish everything. If you'll help the others when it's your turn to work with them, I'll help you study for your tests, Mabel."

"Alright. Thanks."

"We can help each other just as long as ..."

"We each write our own homework!" Jim interrupted, finishing his twin's sentence. "No cheating or copying each other's answers. Isn't that right, Allister?"

That afternoon when school was dismissed, Allister was surprised to see Jessie and Mother standing outside. "Go ahead, son. I'd like to talk with your teacher for a few minutes."

Allister started the walk home, but doubled back. *Talk to my teacher? Why? Am I in trouble?* Sneaking around the back of the school, he crouched under an open window. His mother's voice was coming from various parts of the room while she talked. What was she doing? As much as Allister wanted to look, he didn't dare peek. Mother had better not find out he was eavesdropping.

"Mr. Webster, Jessie's six years old. She's really supposed to be in school this fall, but I'm wondering if it would be better for me to teach her at home this year. Jessie dear, bring me a book. No, Jessie, that's a pencil. Book, bring me a book, dear. Yes, that's right."

"Why do you think you should teach Jessie at home, Mrs. McRuer?" the teacher asked.

Unbelievable! Allister thought. *Mr. Webster completely missed the fact that my little sister has trouble understanding sometimes. I know she has even more difficulty learning.*

"Let me show you something," Mother continued.

Allister heard chalk scrape on a slate.

"Jessie, show me an E," Mother said. "That's right. Show me a J. Very good. Now show me an A. No … an A. No … that's alright, Jessie. We'll do some more letters later. Here's chalk and a slate. Draw me a picture.

"Now, as you can see, Mr. Webster, sometimes she understands and remembers; sometimes she doesn't. You probably have enough beginners to deal with, since this is the first school this area has ever had."

"You can say that for sure," the teacher remarked.

"Jessie is the youngest of my seven children," Mother said. "How many pupils do you have?"

"Sixteen."

"What grades are they in?"

"First, fourth, and eighth. Your boys are sixth/seventh."

"How many are in first grade?"

"Twelve. Ten of them have no schooling; one of those is eleven years old!"

"Oh, my! You do have your hands full."

Mother was quiet for a moment. Then she offered some advice. "They're all farm children, and farm children have to do daily chores. Ask your students to help you keep the room in order. Write daily jobs and assign a student to each job. It'll give them pride in their school and make it easier on you. That way neither you nor I will become Wood Lake School's janitor."

Mr. Webster laughed. "Thanks for cleaning up the room."

"Children who have never been in school, or even a church, usually don't know when it's best to be quiet. Is that true of your students?"

"Oh yes. That's especially true at the beginning of the school day as they come in and right after a recess or dinner break."

"Then won't you need to teach them to enter quietly? Could you make some basic school rules and list them on the board? Go over the rules and make sure everyone knows what to do? Set up consequences if a child doesn't keep a rule?"

"Um, something to try, maybe … You're probably right about Jessie. With my current class, I doubt I could give her the individual attention she'd require."

Hearing the scraping of a chair and footsteps coming towards the open window, Allister bolted across the yard, over a fence, and through the pasture. By the time his mother came out of the building with Jessie in hand, Allister was standing behind a cow. While his mother was shaking hands with the teacher at the schoolhouse door, Allister crept among the herd towards the barn, hoping she hadn't seen him.

When school started the next day, the job and name list on the board was no surprise to Allister. Within a couple of days, his schoolmates had learned to enter the schoolhouse quietly and sit without talking until the teacher had given everyone instructions. Mr. Webster did write six rules on the board as Mother had suggested, but he didn't bother to go over them for the children who couldn't read yet, nor did he set consequences for disobedience. Nonetheless, the chaos of the first few days vanished little by little. As the younger students became used to a daily routine of study and activity, order in their one-room school grew.

Just when Allister was beginning to have hope for his schooling, Father threw a rod into the spokes of his mental "wheels." Once again, his father demonstrated to Allister that his and Jim's education was not first on Mr. McRuer's list of priorities.

chapter three

The Return of the Stooks

"Hey, Allister, come look," Jim shouted from the farmyard one afternoon two weeks after school had started.

Now what? Allister grunted and propped his pitchfork against the barn wall. *Interruptions. Annoying. How am I ever to going to finish my chores and have time to do my homework?* He jogged over to stand next to Jim.

The clanking of the machine Jake and Shalazar were pulling reminded Allister of one he had heard before. It was an exact replica of the equipment that had performed its cutting and binding magic on a wheat field last fall. Allister couldn't help gaping at the gangly contraption.

Father sat in the metal seat of the binder with the horses' reins in his hands and a pleased look on his face. "Allister, Jim, stop standing around. There's work to be done. Wheat harvest starts tomorrow. Allister, run and tell your teacher that you and your brother need to be excused for harvest."

Oh no! Allister thought. *How will Jim and I ever finish the sixth grade if we have to miss so much school?* Groaning, he turned to Jim and muttered, "I'll be right back to help finish our chores."

The next morning, Maggie's colt was put in the pasture with Shalazar so that Maggie could be harnessed with Jake once again. Hitched to the McCormick machine, the team of Clydesdales began their sweep through the fields. While Allister's father and older brothers took turns driving the team, everyone else followed behind, gathering the bound sheaves. Standing the sheaves up to lean with their heads of grain supporting each other, the McRuer family formed stooks, rows of golden pyramids across their fields. Even with Allister and all four of his brothers stooking, they couldn't keep up with the machine. Full days of constantly bending and lifting gave him a royal backache, yet he didn't dare complain. His nineteen-year-old sister, Mary, was stooking along with her brothers. The work was probably just as hard on her as it was on Allister. He was doubly glad that the oat crop had been cut and stooked during the summer.

On the fourth day of stooking, Mary's fiancé, Joe, joined the family in the fields. When the McRuers' wheat crop stood ready for threshing, they drove their binder and wagon over to Joe's to work on his fields. At the end of each workday, they left the machine in the field and rode home in the wagon. After three days, Joe's fields were ready for the threshing crew too.

The following Sunday afternoon, a stranger rode up the lane, dismounted, and tied his horse to the rail near the water trough. Before the stranger got halfway across the farmyard, Allister saw him through a window and ran to alert his mother.

"Do you know who it is?" Mother asked, removing her apron and tucking in a loose strand of her hair.

"I believe it's Reverend Forsythe, an itinerant preacher. The last time I was at St. Matthew's Anglican Church in Cherry Creek to return Reverend Wood's book, the vicar introduced me to this minister."

"Alright, son, seat him in the sitting room. Then go get your father."

Allister opened the front door before the preacher had raised his hand to knock. "Reverend Forsythe, please come in," he said, taking the man's hat. "Have a seat. Mother will be here in a minute, and I'm to get Father. Please make yourself comfortable. I'll be right back." Before the man had any opportunity to respond, Allister had hung the preacher's hat on a hook on the hall tree next to the front door and left the house.

Heading around the house towards the field, he spied his father and his twenty-one-year-old brother, Will, engaged in what appeared to be an argument. Allister's twenty-three-year-old brother, John, stood between them, as if to keep Father and Will apart. Running past a row of the upright pyramids of wheat, Allister arrived in time to hear John say, "Let Will do what he wants, Father. Everything will work out … you'll see."

What does Will want to do? Allister wondered. A cloud of dread settled over him. His father and brothers fell silent as he approached.

"Father, please excuse the interruption," Allister said, "but we have a very important visitor. Mother says to come."

"Alright, son, I'll be there in a minute or two." But Father didn't move. He, John, and Will waited with arms folded across their chests, looking at Allister.

"Ah, um … I'm going now." Turning around, he trotted back across the field.

Fifteen minutes later, Father came in the back door. From a kitchen window, Allister could see John and Will in the farmyard. Apparently still deep into their discussion, John stood with his hand on his younger brother's shoulder. Will was speaking with a frown on his face, hands on hips, and eyes downcast. He was kicking clods of dirt with the toe of a boot. *Ever the negotiator,* Allister thought, watching John. *I wonder what he's trying to talk Will out of this time.*

"Allister, help Mary make some tea, would you?" Mother's voice from the sitting room brought his mind back to their visitor.

Leaving Joe with Mother and Reverend Forsythe in the sitting room, Mary came into the kitchen and filled a kettle from the well water bucket. "Allister, would you go get a jar of raspberry jam from the cellar for me, please?" When the butter, jam, scones, and tea were ready, Mary called everyone into the dining room.

"Reverend Forsythe, the timing of your visit couldn't have been better," Father said after sipping from his cup. "Our daughter, Mary, is soon to be married to young Joe here. Mother and I are wondering if you're available to marry them."

"I believe so," Reverend Forsythe said, smiling. "Have you selected a date yet?"

"The Saturday after Thanksgiving," Mary said, nestling her hand into Joe's. "But I'm not sure where we should have it. I'd like the wedding service to be close to home, because we'll probably have the reception here, won't we, Mother?"

Mother looked at Father and they both nodded.

"How about holding the wedding at Wood Lake School?" Reverend Forsythe suggested.

"Can we do that?" Mary asked.

"Sure. One room schoolhouses serve all kinds of community needs. Just contact your local school board. In fact, I came here today to suggest that we start church services at Wood Lake School. Since I ride to several preaching points in this area, I planned to hold services there every other Sunday morning. I was going to contact a school board member, either Mr. Kempthorne or Mr. Cossar, for permission to start the Sunday after next, if that's agreeable to you," the preacher said, looking at Father.

"Yes, of course."

"Wonderful!" Mother exclaimed. "Maybe now we can start a Sunday school for the children as well."

"That'd be excellent," Reverend Forsythe said. "Who plays the pump organ I saw in your sitting room?"

"I do," Mother said.

"Organ music really adds to a church service," the preacher continued. "The few churches on the Manitoba prairies are rarely blessed with enough hymnals; therefore, few people know the melodies well. A musical instrument would really help the singing. Would you be willing to lend yours to the school and play it for the services, Mrs. McRuer?"

"Yes, I'd love to."

"I'm not sure how to get it to the school …" the preacher paused.

"Don't worry about that," Father said. "We brought it here with us from Lachute, Quebec. Taking it to the school won't be a problem for my sons and me."

"What are you volunteering us for now, Father?" John asked, entering the room with Will, Dan, Jim, and Jessie.

"Having Dan lead the singing in the church services at Wood Lake School Sunday after next," Allister quipped, smiling mischievously at his seventeen-year-old brother.

"Well, I don't know if …" Dan started to sputter.

"Relax, son," Father said, glaring at Allister. "Your voluntary services are only needed to move Mother's organ to the school two Saturdays from now."

"Oh, that's easy!" the sons chorused together.

"Reverend Forsythe, let me introduce you to the rest of my family," Father said, starting with the eldest, John.

With the first rooster crow the next morning, Father shook Allister and Jim awake. "Gotta hustle this morning, boys. We need to be done with chores and breakfast before the threshing machine and crew arrive."

Having already faced one season of threshing during last year's harvest, Allister felt more capable of handling the demands of the long days ahead of him. Squaring his jaw, he followed his family to the waiting fields.

Two hours later, John sent Jim and Allister to the pump in the farmyard to get water for the thirsty threshers. Standing with his brimming buckets, Allister wistfully watched the other children on their way to school.

"Allister, we've got water to deliver," Jim reminded.

Jerked back to reality, Allister grunted. "I know."

"I daydream in school. You wool gather when you're not."

Three days later, both Joe's and the McRuers' harvests were complete. Allister and Jim had helped to stook and thresh hundreds of bushels of wheat and oats.

As Allister settled into his seat the first day back at school, he hoped his tired body wouldn't hinder his brain. *I wonder how long it'll take us to catch up on the two weeks of school we've missed. At least those golden stooks can stop stalking me all night now.*

chapter four

To Become the Heart of the Community

llister scanned the horizon past the bobbing heads of Jake and Maggie as the team pulled the McRuers' wagon full of wheat sacks towards Desford and its grain elevator. After a four-and-a-half-mile trek west along the main road, he hoped to be rewarded with improvements to the small town that he hadn't seen since last fall. When their wagon pulled up next to the elevator, however, Allister could see that there was still no church or school. The town had grown by only a few more houses. He couldn't help thinking, *Good thing we built Wood Lake School on our own property and didn't wait for Desford to build one.*

A bell jingled overhead when Allister and Jim entered Desford's general store ahead of Mother, Mary, and Jessie. This time the McRuers weren't the only customers. Several other women were shopping or visiting. A few children chased each other between the barrels of merchandise. One of the small boys ran up to Allister. It was Georgie, his youngest schoolmate.

"Hi, Allister, come look." Grabbing his hand, Georgie pulled him towards the nearest glass display case. "Aren't they grand?"

Allister bent over to have a look. Brightly painted, metal toy train engines and cars, horses and buggies, along with boys carrying fishing poles, waited on a shelf to go home with a boy or girl. Looking at the prices of the toys, he let out a low whistle. "Yes, Georgie, they're grand and expensive!" *Who has money for toys like these?* Allister wondered.

Glancing at the boy's wistful face, he added, "But it doesn't cost a thing to look, does it?"

Squatting next to Georgie, Allister spent several minutes pointing out specific toys and talking about them.

"Hey, Allister, over here!" Jim called from the other side of the store.

Taking Georgie's hand, Allister led his young friend around the barrels to where Jim was standing in front of some sports equipment. "Look! Baseballs and bats!" Jim said. "Wish we could buy one."

"Let's ask Mother. She gave us some money the last time we came here."

Minutes later, the two were deciding which items to buy as they fingered the quarters she'd given them.

"I'll buy a bat if you'll buy a baseball," Jim suggested.

Allister hesitated. *This store finally has something for sale that I want … books.* "Jim, give me a minute to check on something." Turning, he almost stumbled over Georgie. "Oh, sorry. Forgot you were right beside me. Stay here with Jim. I'll be right back."

Standing at the counter in front of the shelf with the books on it, Allister waited for a clerk. "How much is that book?" he asked, pointing at a book on the top shelf.

"*Tour of the World in Eighty Days*?" the young man asked.

When Allister nodded, the clerk said, "Seventy cents."

"Thank you, sir." Disappointed, Allister glanced at the quarter in his hand, and then stared longingly at the books. *I may not have enough money just now, but someday when I'm old enough to earn a dollar a day on a threshing crew, I'll have enough to buy all the books I want.*

Clearing the lump in his throat, Allister asked the clerk, "Could you please help my brother Jim and me at the sports counter?"

In no time, Jim was walking away with a bat over his shoulder while Allister stuffed a baseball in his pocket. With Georgie close behind them, they approached the candy display case. Jessie was already there with her face practically glued to the glass.

"Georgie, I'll buy you one candy," Allister offered. "Which one do you want?"

The small boy pressed his hands and nose against the glass, fogging it. After several moments, he pointed.

"Oh, you want a peppermint. Alright. My favourite is licorice."

"Jessie, here you are," Jim said, giving her the piece she had previously asked him for— a lemon drop.

As they ambled towards the front of the store to wait for the rest of their family members to complete their purchases, Allister, Jim, Georgie, and Jessie slurped on their sweets.

"Well, did you spend every penny?" Allister asked Jim.

"Of course! Didn't you?"

"No. Still have some. Like to save a little. Might need it later."

"What should we do now? Father, John, Will, and Dan sold our wheat to the Desford elevator. They're here looking through the Sears, Roebuck catalogue."

"Mother and Mary are trying to select material for wedding clothes," Allister added, rolling his eyes. "Think they'll be here awhile."

"I know! Let's see who wants to play some baseball with us, eh?"

Dan, four other boys, and one other girl needed little urging to join their game. No one really knew the rules of the game, so Dan helped them make a few up as they played. Because Jessie couldn't hit the ball, and her limp made it hard for her to run between bases, Jim was her stand-in. After he hit for her and ran to the sack that served as first base, Jessie stood on the base. Part way through the game, Mother came out to gather her family for their picnic on the grass near the town pump.

"What did you buy?" Allister asked Mother while they were eating.

"Material for Mary's wedding dress and some fabric for towels and pillows to put in her hope chest."

"What did you decide to order, Father?" Jim asked.

"Another wagon, a buggy for Mother, and a buggy harness for Shalazar."

"Did you order anything, John?" Dan asked.

"Yes, a horse-drawn mower. No more scythe swinging!"

"Yay!" Allister couldn't help letting out a whoop.

"Hey, Will, what were you looking for in the catalogue?" Jim asked.

Will glanced at John and then at Father.

"Go ahead, Will," Father said. "Tell the rest of the family about your plans."

"During this year's harvest, I earned enough money on the threshing crews to pay the fee for my own homestead claim," Will said. "So I ordered a steel walking plow."

That's what they were arguing about last month! Allister thought. He asked, "Have you selected the claim you want, Will?"

"Yes."

"Where is it?"

"An hour's ride north of Cherry Creek."

Allister gasped. *Hurrah! Will's moving out! He won't be around to needle me. But miles north of Cherry Creek? That's far away.* Keeping his thoughts to himself, Allister asked, "When are you planning on moving there, Will?"

Will hesitated. Silently gazing at John and then at prairie land off in the distance, he gulped and fidgeted. "Sometime next spring … March or April," he finally answered.

John let out a whoop, slapping his brother on the back. "Good decision!"

That's what John was trying to persuade Will to do. John must have suggested Will wait until spring, Allister thought. Out loud he asked, "Does the homestead have any buildings on it? Or a well?"

"No, neither."

"What a lot of work!"

"More than you'll ever be willing to do, Aaalliiisss!" Will snarled.

Allister studied the grass leaf he was twirling in his hands. Mulling over the retort that was ready to spring from his tongue, he was silent a moment. *Why does Will always shoot me down like that? He's assuming he'll never get any help from me with the difficult task ahead of him.* Rising to his feet, Allister said as evenly as he could muster, "I do as much work as anybody else in this family, and you know it!"

Stuffing his clenched fists in his pockets and gritting his teeth, Allister stomped east along the road, heading home alone. Scenes of his efforts to knock Will's meanness down his throat flashed through Allister's mind. *In the boxcar just before we arrived in Cherry Creek, my swing at Will almost landed me on the railroad tracks under the car's wheels. If Jim hadn't grabbed me, I'd have been killed.* Allister took his fists out of his pockets. *Our first night at the homestead, I tried again to punch Will's lights out. I ended up face down in the mud.* Allister increased his pace to a jog. *Will is taller, stronger, and nine years older than me! It's not fair. It's never fair.*

With the thunder of his internal storm roaring in his head, Allister barely heard his mother calling to him to wait and ride with the rest of the family. Deciding to ignore her, Allister thought about Reverend Wood's advice. *The vicar was right. He told me to not let Will get my goat. Well, I can't let Will see that he has.* When Allister rounded a bend and figured his family could no longer see him, he punched the air. With each sweep of a fist, he released his pent-up anger, hurt, and frustration. He dug his heels into the dirt until he was flying past prairie grass. A river gushed from his eyes down his face and filled his mouth with the taste of salt. Allister ran until his sides ached.

Slowing to a walk, he gasped for breath. *Time alone,* he thought. *That's what I need. With six siblings I rarely get that. Six? All too soon it'll be four. I never really thought about anyone leaving except Mary, after her marriage to Joe. And now Will is planning to move the other side of Cherry Creek! It might as well be to the moon, for all we'll see of him. But that'll be good ... for me!* Relief flooded Allister's heart at the thought. The exercise had helped him expel some of his emotions as well.

Off in the distance he saw the ravine that lay west of their homestead. As he approached it, he turned off the road and trekked up the creek's bank towards Turtle Mountain. Clambering over boulders and winding his way between trees, he reached a lake on the top of the mountain. A dock stretched over the water. Allister ambled along the length of planks and sat beside the boat that rested upside down near the end of the dock. Removing his boots, he wiggled his toes in the cold wet. September wasn't really a good time for a swim, but the remainder of the glowing yellows, flaming reds, and sombre rust of the shoreline woods reflected warmly on the glassy surface around him. *God, You made such a beautiful world,* he prayed. *You probably don't like Will's meanness either.*

As the sun set, Allister returned to the farm and went to the barn to do his chores. When he finished, he entered the house. The rest of the family had just eaten supper and were leaving to do their share of the animal care.

Mother looked up. Upon seeing Allister, she smiled and her furrowed brow relaxed. Without a word, she dished up stew, sliced some bread, and set the food on the table.

Allister went to the wash basin, pumped some water, and washed his hands and face before sitting on the bench at the kitchen table. "Thank you, Mother."

Although no one, not even Jessie, spoke to him, John put his hand on Allister's shoulder as he headed for the back door. Allister waited until everyone left except Mother and Jessie. Then he bowed his head and said a silent grace. When he raised his head, Mother was sitting across the table, sipping a cup of tea and studying him.

"Where you go?" Jessie asked, tapping his arm.

"Turtle Mountain."

"What you do there?"

"I sat on a dock over a lake, took off my boots, and wiggled my toes in the water."

"Why?"

Hmmm. That's a very good question, Allister thought. "To cool off."

"Cool off? You hot?"

"Yes. Will made me hot!"

"Oh … Willie bad boy!" Jessie said, frowning with her lip stuck way out and her arms folded across her chest. Shaking her head, she added, "Not kind! I love you, Allister."

Jessie wrapped her arms around him. He hugged her back. *For a girl who is slow*, Allister thought, *sometimes Jessie is SO smart!* "Thank you, Jessie," he said with a lump rising in his throat and tears rimming his eyes. His mother reached across the table and squeezed his hand.

When Allister woke up the next morning, he could hear Mother and Mary hurrying about the kitchen. Dressing quickly in work clothes, he ran downstairs.

"Allister, today is our first church service at Wood Lake School," Mother said. "Be dressed in your cleanest clothes and ready to ride over by 10:15 a.m. Service starts at 11:00."

Pausing at the bottom of the stairs, Allister peeked into the dining room. Mother's mantel clock on the top of the hutch showed 7:30 a.m. *Uh oh, I overslept. Better hustle.* As he hurried to the outhouse and then to do his chores, he reminded himself to think about what he was doing. There was no point in hurrying if it meant that he might have to retrace his steps to do something twice. "Do it right the first time" was his personal motto. After finishing, he bolted across the farmyard just as his family was sitting down to breakfast. Joining them, he waited until Mother said the blessing over the meal before he got up to wash his hands and face. By the time Allister sat down, the rest of the family had finished their breakfast, and there was little food still on the table.

At 10:15, everybody was ready to get in the wagon for the short ride to the school. When the McRuers drove up to the paddock fence behind the school, Allister could see two other teams and the pastor's horse tied to the railing.

Inside the building, Thomas was helping Reverend Forsythe position a short podium on the teacher's desk. Between the two windows along the left wall sat Mother's pump organ. Father led his family to the row of desks nearest the organ. Three families sat whispering and waiting for the service to start. The younger children soon tired of sitting and chased each other around the room.

"Allister, Jim, help me play a game with the children outside until it's time to start," Mary suggested. "Mother needs to get the hymns ready."

While they played the circle game of Duck, Duck, Goose on the grass in the yard, Allister could hear the strains of "Holy, Holy, Holy" coming from inside the schoolhouse.

More families in their wagons and buggies pulled up near the building. Thomas came out. Lifting the school bell high in the fall breeze, he rang it loud and long. It was time. When Allister re-entered the room, he was surprised to see all the desks and benches filled. *Word must have gotten out*, he mused as he looked around the room. *Now that we have a place to meet, our neighbours don't want to miss a service.* Allister smiled.

"Welcome, friends and neighbours," the pastor greeted his new congregation. "Please stand while I read the call to worship: '*O sing unto the Lord a new song: sing unto the Lord, all the earth. Sing unto the Lord, bless his name; shew forth his salvation from day to day. Declare his glory among the heathen, his wonders among all people.*[1] Let's pray."

Reverend Forsythe bowed his head and waited until all was quiet. In his prayer, he thanked God for all of His blessings, including the harvest just completed.

"Let's sing this song together," he said, raising his head and pointing at the song on the board. "First, let's read it together. Then Mrs. McRuer will play the tune. When she plays it a second time, we'll all sing. It's wonderful to have an instrument to lead us!"

Soon everyone was singing lustily, even the children.

"Now take a minute to greet and shake the hand of a neighbour standing near you."

When the hubbub died down, Thomas walked to the front of the room and read the Old Testament lesson from the Bible.

"Please remain standing for the reading of the New Testament lesson."

Mabel, Allister's schoolmate, walked to the front and, standing next to the pastor, read from Matthew 13 a story that Jesus told. It was about a farmer who sowed a field with wheat seed. Later his workers noticed weeds in the field. They asked their boss if they should go and pull up the weeds.

Reverend Forsythe asked Mabel to pause the reading. Looking at the farmers before him, he asked, "What do you think the farmer in the story answered?"

All the men in the congregation shook their heads. "No," several mumbled.

Reverend Forsythe asked Mabel to continue the reading. While she was reading, Allister thought about the topic of the story. Until today, he hadn't realized that the Bible had anything to say about wheat fields or farming.

When Mabel sat down, the pastor started his sermon by asking his audience, "Jesus was right to say, 'no, not now, but we will separate the weeds from the wheat at harvest time,' wasn't he? But why wait 'til then?"

"Because early on, the weeds and the wheat are the same colour," John called out.

Chuckles rippled across the families.

"Ah, a man of experience," the pastor remarked, smiling and nodding. "That's right. While the wheat and the weeds are growing, both are green. Only at harvest can a farmer truly tell which is wheat and which is weed ... one golden, the other still green."

Allister mulled over the point the pastor made. *True. A farmer must wait months to know for sure which plants are good and which are not. Not me. I don't want to wait for things to change. But I haven't been able to stop Will's taunts. Reverend Wood, my vicar friend in Cherry Creek, told me not to give in to Will's trap of pushing me into losing control. He just laughs when he knows he's succeeded. Guess I need a farmer's kind of patience. It would be better if I waited for things to change between us, but I wonder how long that will take. Waiting is so hard.*

Reading further from Matthew 13, the pastor emphasized the ultimate fate of the weeds. He concluded with a suggestion. "Consider which you are, wheat or weed, in God's field. Have you allowed God's enemy to sow evil in your heart, or have you allowed God's Son, Jesus, to sow His good seed, His truth, in your heart?"

After a poignant pause, Reverend Forsythe said, "Everyone please stand for our closing prayer and benediction."

As Allister stood, he thought about the story and the pastor's questions. *I want God's truth in my heart. Doing things my own way certainly hasn't worked. I wonder what else the Bible says about everyday life. Like Reverend Wood always tells me, read to find out.*

"Before you go, I'd like to invite you all for a special service Thanksgiving Day here at 10:00 a.m. Our next regular worship will be two weeks from today."

Families took their time leaving. Since most rarely saw each other, they enjoyed the opportunity to visit, something everyone needed. With Jessie in hand, Mother and Mary wandered from group to group, chatting. Jim chased the other children around all the buildings. John, Will, and Dan lolled about, visiting with other young farmers and eyeing the few young girls with their families. Father stood next to his Clydesdales, talking with two old timers, swapping stories. Allister sat on the top rail of the paddock fence, content to people watch. *Donating this land and helping to build this schoolhouse was the best thing we McRuers could have done for our neighbours.*

Thomas and Reverend Forsythe were the last ones out of the building. Locking the door, the pastor greeted a few people before mounting his horse to follow Thomas and Caroline's wagon down the trail. This Sunday their pastor was going to have dinner with Thomas' family before riding to lead the worship service for his next congregation that afternoon.

chapter five

Wedding Bells

"Come on, wake up." Someone was shaking Allister's shoulder. He hadn't heard the rooster crow. Thinking it couldn't be time to get up yet, he groaned and rolled over. But the shaker didn't quit. "Allister, you've got to get up now!"

He opened his eyes. The persistent shaker was his oldest brother, John. Allister sat up and dropped his bare feet to the cold, wood floor. "What's the matter, John? It's still dark outside."

"That may be," his brother grunted. "But Mary's getting married today. Got to get all the chores finished before breakfast. Roast the Angus steer we butchered yesterday. Remember?"

Allister did remember. He thought about all the work that had already been done. A week prior, Father and Dan had built two extra plank tables to set on sawhorses, and four extra benches to seat the guests at the reception. John and Will had gone hunting and brought home a dozen geese and ducks. Allister had worked with the rest of his family to pluck and stuff enough down to make two new pillows for Mary and Joe's wedding present. *Those pillows are definitely softer than the one I'm using. Mine is stuffed with straw.*

Several days before the wedding, Mother, Mary, and Caroline had spent all day in the kitchen measuring, beating, and baking. They told Allister they were working on Mary's wedding cake. That evening, Allister couldn't believe his eyes. A white, three-tiered cake sat in the middle of the dining room table, making him drool. Remembering the spicy sweetness of his mother's fruitcake and the richness of her creamy butter icing, Allister wondered if he could get away with snitching a bite. "Better not," he told himself.

After school yesterday, Allister and Jim took turns keeping Jessie busy and out from underfoot so that Mother and Mary could clean and polish the schoolhouse. Allister knew that Dan had already done his share of Jessie-care during school hours while the two women had done the same to the McRuer home.

Early in the morning of Mary's big day and after chores, Allister and Jim helped John chop kindling for the fire pit Will and Father dug. The twins watched their father set up the large wooden supports on each side of the pit before he lit the kindling. Next came the fresh beef skewered onto a long, metal pipe. Father and Will placed the pipe's ends in the Y of the supports. Fitting a crank into one end of the skewer pipe and handing Dan a pair of leather gloves, Father said, "Yours is the first watch over this beef roast. Keep the fire burning. Turn the meat a little bit every few minutes. The crank will get very hot, so be sure to use the gloves. In a couple of hours, John will relieve you. Mother will bring out your breakfast."

Father glanced at the kindling pile that Allister and Jim had been stacking. "That's enough for now, boys. Let's eat. There will be plenty of other tasks for you to do this morning."

After breakfast, Mother, Mary, and Jessie worked on the remainder of the meal for the wedding reception, pressing Allister and Jim into the family-fetchers service. Jam, extra eggs, onions, carrots, jars of canned corn and tomatoes, potatoes, wheat flour, and cornmeal all had to be brought up from the cellar. While Will chopped more kindling for the roasting pit outside, Allister and Jim hauled drinking water into the house. With only a few hours left before the wedding, Allister fretted, *Will we get everything done in time?*

Together, Allister and Jim loaded the skid with the fall foliage that had been gathered from Turtle Mountain and had been hanging from the kitchen ceiling beams to dry. Allister walked behind to monitor the load while Jim dragged it to the schoolhouse. Waiting at the door was Caroline. After she had helped them transfer the branches to the platform at the front of the room, she shooed Allister and Jim home. "I'll take it from here. You two hustle back. I'm sure you have other things to get ready."

When Allister and Jim returned with the empty skid to the back door, Dan was busy rearranging the kitchen furniture. "Hey, Allister, Jim," he called, "bring in the extra tables and benches. Then Father wants you two to get Shalazar ready."

Before Allister headed to the barn, he suggested they grab something to eat. Since there would be no time to sit down for a noon meal together, Mother had set out bread, butter, and bowls for soup for everyone to eat whenever he or she had time.

"Alright, Allister … eat, but don't take all day," Dan lectured. "It is already past noon."

The grooming and harnessing of Shalazar didn't exactly go smoothly. While Allister and Jim applied brushes and curry combs to the horse's sides, the gelding moved restlessly. When it was time to put the bit in the horse's mouth, he wouldn't stop tossing his head.

"Grab his ear and hold his head down," Jim instructed.

After Allister succeeded, Jim thrust his finger into the side of Shalazar's mouth to force him to open it. In a split second, Jim shoved the bit in and slipped the top of the bridle over the other of Shalazar's ears. "Alright, Allister, let go."

Jim looped the leather over the remaining ear and managed to buckle the throat latch before Shalazar resumed his head tossing.

"Wow," Allister commented, "that was a tussle. Hope he behaves better between the buggy shafts."

As two o'clock approached, Caroline came over to help Mary and Jessie get ready, and Mother hustled Allister and his brothers into clean clothes. While they stood in the farmyard waiting for Jessie, Allister could see Reverend Forsythe unlocking the schoolhouse door, and Joe entering behind him. Father led Shalazar out of the barn and hitched him to their brand new buggy.

Allister watched the horse fidget. *I hope that horse behaves—especially today!*

Walking with his brothers towards the school, Allister smiled up at Jessie as she rode on John's shoulders. His little sister's soft brown hair was tied into miniature ponytails with red ribbons. On her head she wore a knit, green and brown tam with a red pompom. Her new dress was light green. Around her waist was tied a wide sash and bow of the family's Scottish tartan, a forest green and bright red plaid on a field of brown. Allister reached up and squeezed her hand. "Jessie, you look like a little Scottish wedding lassie."

Jessie's excited giggle rippled through the autumn sunshine.

Entering the schoolhouse behind his brothers, Allister's mouth dropped open. The colourful fall leaf branches that he and Jim had brought were fastened to the aisle sides of their school desks, the end of the bookcase, and the sides of the blackboard. Additional branches brightened the top of Mother's pump organ and the teacher's desk. The yellow, gold, orange, brown, rusty red, and maroon hues made the room look like the woods around a clearing on Turtle Mountain in September.

While John and Will remained near the schoolhouse door to act as ushers, Allister, Jim, and Jessie filed to the front bench and sat down. Jim held Jessie's hand until it would be time for her to join Mary at the back of the room. Dan stood near the organ and played on his harmonica every lively tune he had ever taught himself. Thomas took the school bell from the teacher's desk and exited the building. Through the window near his seat, Allister could see Thomas ring the bell from the middle of the schoolyard. Families came in and whispered to each other after they were seated.

In the front of the room next to Reverend Forsythe, Joe tugged at his collar and shuffled his feet. Alternately, he rubbed the top of one shoe on the back of the other pant leg, glanced out the open schoolhouse door, or stared at the pendulum clock ticking on the back wall.

It's time to start the wedding, Allister thought, turning to peek at the clock. *Where are Mother and Father? Where's Mary?* When he heard the clop of hooves and the crunch of wheels on dirt and pebbles, Allister breathed a sigh of relief.

Joe stopped fidgeting, and everyone became quiet. At the sudden clatter of hooves and the shout of his father, Allister jumped up and ran to the door, just in time to see their new buggy careening at break-neck speed from the schoolyard onto the road, heading west. Father ran past him into the building. "Joe," he yelled from the back of the room, "Shalazar's run off with your bride. Better go get her!"

Eyes wide with alarm, Joe looked at Reverend Forsythe. "Take my horse!" he offered. "Be quick!"

Joe tore out of the building and vaulted onto its back. Jerking the reins loose from the paddock railing and reining its head around, Joe dug his heels into the startled animal's flanks. Lying along the horse's neck, he slapped his mount with the ends of the reins. Horse and anxious rider disappeared into the cloud of dust that rose behind the runaway buggy.

Allister ran to the road and looked west. Jim jogged up and stood beside him. Minutes ticked by as they waited. Out of the corner of his eye, he saw everyone come out of the schoolhouse. "I've heard of another fellow running off with the bride, but never a horse," wisecracked one man.

The wind whipped away the dust following the buggy. Grabbing his brother's arm, Allister shouted, "Look, Joe's almost caught up to her! Now he's got Shalazar's rein."

Jim jumped and whooped.

As he watched Joe turn the runaway around, Allister let his breath out with a whoosh. He shook his head and muttered, "That dumb horse. Had a feeling he'd be up to no good today!"

Father joined Allister in the middle of the road. "Father, what happened?"

"I'd just helped Mother out of the buggy. Then when I reached up to help Mary out, Shalazar took off!"

"Something spook him?" Jim asked.

"Don't know what would have, out here," Father said.

A short time later, Joe returned on the pastor's horse at a trot, leading Shalazar, who was still hitched to the buggy. Mary looked a little scared; her hair and sash were askew. At the door of the school, Joe dismounted and handed the reins of the preacher's horse to Jim. Standing in front of Shalazar, Joe held the panting, wild-eyed gelding with a firm grip on his bridle. After Father helped Mary out of the buggy, everyone except Father, Caroline, Mary, Joe, and Allister went back inside.

"You go in, Allister," Caroline said. "I'll make sure Mary is set to rights."

After one more glance at Mary, Allister scurried to his seat. "Jim, it's time to send Jessie to Etta in the back of the room."

Several minutes passed. When Joe re-entered the schoolhouse and walked towards the front of the room, several men clapped him on the back. "Nice work, Joe … Great rescue … Glad Mary's safe."

Smiling and looking relieved, Joe and his best man, Dan, took their places next to Reverend Forsythe once more. Mother returned to her seat at the organ and began to slowly play "Largo" by Handel. Etta, wearing a light brown dress with a Scottish tartan sash and bow, led Jessie down the aisle to the front of the room, helping her scatter bright fall leaves from the basket hanging from her arm. Mary's matron of honour, Caroline, wearing a simple dark-brown dress, followed behind the two girls. When Mary entered the room on Father's arm, Mother sounded the first seven notes of the "Bridal Chorus" from the opera *Lohengrin* by Wagner, and everyone stood up.

As his sister walked towards the front of the room, Allister turned around to have a good look at her. Mary had straightened the Scottish tartan sash that she wore over her long, dark- green dress. The ringlets of her brown hair hung neatly coiled half way down her back. On her head, a circle of fall leaves formed a colourful crown. With a slight blush on her cheeks, and her blue eyes sparkling, Mary smiled non-stop. Allister thought his sister to be the loveliest bride he'd ever seen.

The wedding service proceeded without another hitch.

"And now I present to you for the first time, Mr. and Mrs. Joseph Boyd," the Reverend announced.

Bride and groom turned around to face their families and friends. Mary tucked her hand in the crook of Joe's arm. The couple beamed as they accepted the congregation's applause. Father and Mother then joined Joe and Mary, inviting all to the McRuer home for the wedding reception.

As everyone filed out of the schoolhouse, the wedding party clustered around a large Bible on the teacher's desk. Allister lingered near the door long enough to watch Reverend Forsythe write in the front of the book.

Allister's mother walked towards him. "Mother, what are they doing?"

"Signing their names in Joe's family Bible, stating that they were witnesses to Joe's marriage to Mary. If you look in our family Bible, you'll see the signing of your father's marriage to me."

"Like a family history book?"

His mother smiled. "I've never thought of it that way, but yes, you're right."

As the families left the schoolhouse, all took some wheat from John's and Will's baskets. Forming a line on either side of the exit path, their family members and friends got ready to shower the bride and groom as they came out. Allister grabbed two fistfuls. Jim copied him. Standing opposite each other in the lines, Allister and then Jim pelted the couple when they walked by. Joe threw his arms around Mary. "Allister, Jim, take it easy. Tossing wheat is supposed to represent a wish for God's blessing on our new life together, not a chance to attack us."

"Oops, sorry," Allister said with a grimace.

Jim just laughed. "Relax, Joe. We're just having a bit of fun."

Father led Shalazar out of the paddock and held him as Joe helped Mary into the buggy. When Joe was seated and had a firm grip on the reins, Father let go of the horse and led the rest of his family to Joe's wagon. A line of wagons followed into the McRuers' farmyard.

Jim and Allister were put in charge of Shalazar. They led him to the back of the yard, unhitched him, removed his harness, and rubbed the still-sweaty animal down. "Let's tie him up in his stall," Jim suggested. "We don't really have time to walk him until he's calmed down and cooled off. He shouldn't eat or drink anything until he has. We'll have to see to him later."

"You're right," Allister said. "Mother said she needs us to help serve our guests."

As the twins walked across the farmyard towards the house, they were surprised to see a pair of Mounties ride up. "Hello, young masters!"

Recognizing the brogue of Constable MacDonald, Allister smiled and waved.

"Good afternoon, sirs," Jim said. "Here to see Father, I'll bet! I'll get him."

As Jim ran into the house, Allister offered to water their horses. While he was getting a bucket, Mother came out.

"Gentlemen," she said, "you're just in time to join us for our daughter Mary's wedding meal. How nice of you to honour us in this manner!"

The Mounties looked at each other in surprise.

"Well, actually, ma'am," Constable MacDonald admitted, "we just came to buy one or two of your Angus."

"That you are welcome to do," Mother said, "after you've tasted our roasted beef and had a piece of wedding cake!"

"Oh, alright, Mrs. McRuer, you've tempted us enough," the other constable said. "Glad to join the festivities."

The men dismounted and unsheathed their rifles. Handing the reins of their horses to Jim, MacDonald said, "Please loosen the girths and tie our mounts up in one of yoor stalls … that's a good lad."

Father came out as Mother led the Mounties to the back door.

"Ay, sir, greetings from our North West Mounted Police post," Constable MacDonald said. "Come today to buy some beef from yoo, but the good wife here has summoned us to taste a bit 'o beef first."

"Yes, of course," Father said, "you're most welcome."

"Mr. and Mrs. McRuer, may I introduce Constable Smith to yoo?"

After the three had shaken hands, the Mounties asked for a lockable storage space for their firearms. Father handed Constable MacDonald the key to an empty grain bin.

Upon entering the kitchen, Allister hurried to wash his hands and put on an apron. He couldn't help drooling over the plates full of food he delivered to their guests. The slices of roasted beef, a pile of mashed potatoes, corn and egg casserole with stewed tomato topping, and a slice of Mother's fresh-baked bread looked delicious.

The Mounties followed Father and Mother into the dining room. When Allister brought the men their plates, they were sitting as special guests of the wedding party.

After everyone had been served, John, Will, Jim, and Allister filled their plates and went upstairs to sit on their beds to eat. Their pioneer home was overflowing with guests.

"Come down, boys," Mother called from the bottom of the stairs some time later. "It's time for Joe and Mary to cut the cake."

After the couple had fed each other samples, Caroline took over cutting tier by tier. She made sure everyone got a piece of Mother's moist, sweet, spice-filled fruitcake.

"Ah, an honourable Scottish tradition," Constable MacDonald commented as he tasted it.

After everyone had eaten a piece, John opened all the sitting room windows, opened the front door, and cranked up Mother's graphophone. "A wedding dance out front is about to start," he announced.

Taking his cue, Joe led Mary outside. He clumsily directed his wife around the yard while the strains of a waltz blared through the horn of the music machine. After Joe and Mary had made a full circuit of the yard, Father and Mother and other couples joined in. All five brothers took turns cranking the music box, playing again and again their single cylinder of waltzes.

While everyone else continued the dance, Father called Allister and Jim aside. "Take these ropes and go catch the two steers. Our Mountie friends have a long ride ahead of them, and they wish to get going."

Dashing across the farmyard, Jim and Allister climbed over the fence and ran to catch the seven-month-old Angus. The cattle came along readily enough until Allister tried to lead his away from the barn. Bawling and pulling against the rope around its neck, the steer voiced his displeasure at being separated from the herd.

After retrieving their weapons and paying Mr. McRuer for their beef-on-the-hoof, the Mounties thanked their hostess for the wonderful meal and mounted their horses. Each constable fastened the rope of one steer to his saddle, half leading and half dragging their Angus prizes along.

"Don't worry, Allister," John said. "When the farm is out of sight, they'll go easily."

"Good thing those steers don't know what's at end of their trip," Jim said with a wry grin.

chapter six

A Cry in the Night

As Allister and Jim stood with their family watching the Mounties ride off, Joe tapped Mr. McRuer on the arm. "Sir, Mary and I should be leaving soon. We'd like to be home before dark."

"I'll see if Mary needs any help," Mother said.

"Help you with your team, Joe," Father offered.

Allister's heart sank. *I'm not in any hurry for Mary to leave.*

Glancing at Allister, Father paused. "You and Jim better go to the kitchen and get started on the clean-up."

Jim scuffed his shoes and grinned. "Guess Father wants to talk to Joe without us around."

Back in the house, Allister pumped pots full of wash water, and Jim stoked the stove. Dan and Jessie soon came to help, and the four of them collected all the dirty dishes. Several of Mother's women friends washed and dried the dishes while Allister and Jim put things away and Dan helped Jessie wipe tables. John and Will removed the extra plank tables, sawhorses, and benches. Etta, Caroline's oldest daughter, swept the dining room and kitchen floors.

When they were almost finished, Mary came downstairs. She had wrapped her braided hair around her head and was dressed in a garment she usually wore to do farm work. She was carrying a wooden crate of clothes. "Allister," she called through the hubbub, "please go help Mother."

At the top of the stairs, Mother handed him a neatly folded quilt and gave it one last loving pat. He smiled, remembering the low hum of her treadle sewing machine while she worked the colourful pieces during the night watches after everyone else had gone to bed. On top of the quilt, she laid the two pillows the family had made. "Put these in the basket that's next to the wash tub and give it to Joe," she said. "And ask John and Will to carry down Mary's hope chest."

"Mother, I wish she didn't have to go," Allister frowned.

"I know, son. We'll all miss her," his mother agreed. "She is the first to leave home."

Hugging his armload on his way down the stairs, Allister reminisced. *Mary's been like a second mother to me. Always helped me with my reading. Encouraged me to do well in school. Will I be able to manage as well without her?*

Reluctantly, Allister handed Joe his mother's wedding gifts. Finding his older brothers sitting on the pile of lumber beside the barn, Allister delivered Mother's request. While John and Will carried out the now-heavy hope chest, Mother packed an additional basket with some eggs, biscuits, and a small, lidded pot stuffed with butter and leftover roast beef. "Jim, Allister, go get a chicken crate," she said. "Let's give Joe and Mary a couple of our hens. Put in a sack of the cracked corn, too."

All too soon, Joe and Mary had all her things and the family's wedding gifts loaded into his wagon. John lifted Jessie onto his shoulder before he told her to wave goodbye. After all, Mary had been Jessie's second mother and roommate all of her life. When she finally understood that Mary was gone, Allister figured that Jessie would be distraught.

After the newlyweds left, Mother and Father said goodbye to their remaining guests. Wagons fanned out across the prairie into the deepening purple shadows.

There wasn't a whole lot of time to ponder events. His brothers had already gone into the house to change into their work clothes. Wedding day or not, evening chores still had to be done.

When Allister exited the barn that evening, white flakes fluttered into his hair and eyebrows and melted on his eyelashes. The winter season's first snow was silently falling.

Shortly, after a late supper, John came back into the kitchen, carrying a sleeping girl.

"Where was she?" Mother asked.

"In the sitting room. Found her curled up on the settee."

"Take her upstairs, would you, son? Be up in a minute to put her to bed."

Allister followed John upstairs and got himself ready for bed. He needed some time alone. Staring through the darkness of their empty bedroom out the window at the gently falling snow would give him some space for his musings. *I hope Mary will be happy in her new home,* Allister thought before he drifted off to sleep. *It's Jessie's first night alone in her room. I hope she won't be afraid.*

———◆———

"Ah, ah, ah, aaaah!"

Allister felt Jim sit up in bed. "What's that sound?" he whispered.

"Wha, ah, ah, aaaah!"

Allister sat up too. It wasn't coming from the window. Louder and louder. It was coming from Jessie's room.

The door to Mother and Father's room burst open. In her nightgown with her long, single braid flying behind her, Mother ran in her bare feet to Jessie's bedroom. Right behind her were the five brothers. When Allister peeked in, he saw that Mother had lit the lamp on the dresser and was sitting on the bed, holding their lonely, frightened girl. "I'll stay with her until she falls asleep again," Mother said. "Going to take some time for her to get use to no Mary. You boys go back to bed."

As he climbed back onto the squeaky, iron-framed, double bed he shared with Jim, Allister muttered, "Guess I'm not the only one who already misses Mary."

"Me too," Jim said. "Goodnight, Allister."

"Goodnight, Jim."

chapter seven

School on Sunday?

Whoever heard of school on Sunday? Allister thought when his mother announced she would start a class for children the following Sunday. *I wonder what we're going to study.*

At the sound of the school bell on the morning of the first Sunday school class, Allister, Jim, and Jessie climbed into the buggy for the ride over to the schoolhouse. John maintained a firm grip on Shalazar's reins until Jim had gotten out and had a hold of the horse's bridle. Allister lifted Jessie out and took her by the hand into the school. Inside it was pleasantly warm because Mother had gone early to light firewood in the barrel stove.

Allister led Jessie to the front bench so they could sit next to his schoolmates, Georgie, Emily, Charlie, and Etta.

After a few minutes, Jim squeezed in beside Allister, whispering, "John's locked Shalazar and the buggy in the schoolyard paddock and walked home. He says Mother should be the one to drive Mr. Antsy home."

Allister grinned and nodded. "Good idea."

Two more children came in and shyly stood at the back of the room, holding hands. Mother smiled and beckoned for them to sit with the rest of the children.

"My name is Mrs. McRuer. I'm your Sunday school teacher. Let's get everybody's name, alright? Allister, you come to the board and write them for me," she said, handing him a piece of chalk. Pointing at Jim, she said, "We'll start with you."

While Allister was writing, an older teenager came in and sat in the back. Mother stopped and turned towards to him.

"Don't mind me, ma'am," he said. "I'm Alex, Sally and Gilbert's older brother. Our parents asked me to bring them in the wagon, since we live some miles from here."

Mother smiled. "Nice to meet you, Alex. Thank you for bringing your brother and sister. You're welcome to participate, if you'd like to."

When everyone's name was written, Allister returned to his seat, and his mother explained that they would be learning something about God and some of the things He did in the very beginning.

Mrs. McRuer started their lesson with a chorus that she had written on the board. After she helped the children learn the words, she played its melody on the pump organ. Soon the children were singing, "All things bright and beautiful, all creatures great and small, all things wise and wonderful, The Lord God made them all."

"This song talks about a creature," Mrs. McRuer said. "Charlie, do you know what a creature is?"

"Is it an animal?" Charlie guessed.

"Yes, it is. Who made the animals, Sally?"

"God did."

"That's right. Now I'm going to read a story from the Bible's first book, Genesis."

Allister's mother opened their big family Bible that lay on the podium on the teacher's desk. She read from Genesis 1, *"In the beginning God created the heaven and the earth."*[2]

In Quebec, we had Bible lessons as part of our schoolwork every day. Here in Manitoba, we don't. Allister pondered as he listened. *I think I understand why Mother wants to start a Sunday school.*

His mother continued, *"And God said, Let there be light: and there was light. And God saw the light, that it was good: and God divided the light from the darkness."*[3]

Mother stopped reading to ask a question. "Gilbert, what were the first two things that God made?"

"The heaven and ..."

"The earth!" Georgie blurted.

"That's right. Georgie, thank you for helping Gilbert, but give him a little more time to think of the answer. If I ask, 'Who can help Gilbert remember?' then you can help your schoolmate answer. Alright, Georgie?"

The small boy nodded.

"When God saw the light, what did He say about it, Etta?"

"That it was good!"

"Yes, that's correct. Children, you're excellent listeners."

While Mother carefully read and questioned the children to check their understanding and attention, Allister thought about his brother John and how he was so different from both Will and Father. *Will finds fault with everyone, especially me, for some reason. And Father hardly ever praises anybody, but John always does. Now I can see who he copies. Both Mother and John praise every effort, big or little. Thank you, God, for Mother and John.*

She continued reading, *"And the earth brought forth grass, and herb yielding seed after his kind, and the tree yielding fruit, whose seed was in itself, after his kind: and God saw that it was good."*[4]

Mother paused and then read those sentences again. "We have a lot of grass here on the prairie, don't we?"

Everybody nodded.

"How did it get here? Did the old timers bring it?"

There was a loud guffaw from the back of the room. Some of the children giggled.

"No," Gilbert said, "God put it here even before the Indians came."

"So God was here before the Indians and certainly before any French or English people came," Allister commented. *Am I right, then, to be so afraid of how things will go for me? Maybe, just maybe, southwestern Manitoba isn't the end of the earth. My family hasn't left God behind in Quebec, after all.*

"That's right, Allister," Mother smiled and nodded.

She continued. "When the Bible says that the herb, that's a plant, yields seed after his kind, what does that mean? If your father plants wheat seeds, will he get tomatoes?"

More giggles.

"Alright, Charlie, what does 'seed after his kind' mean?"

"A wheat seed makes wheat," the boy said.

"Tomato seed make tomato," Jessie piped up.

Mother smiled broadly. Jessie had helped plant tomato seeds in window boxes last spring and then had watched those plants grow in the garden all summer to make big, ripe, red tomatoes. Allister was surprised his little sister remembered.

"What about a tree? If a farmer plants an acorn, will he get an elm tree?"

Ten heads shook "No!"

"What did God say about the earth He had made, Jim?"

"It was good."

"Yes, and it is! Now think about all the things that we just read and talked about. Allister and Jim, please give everyone a slate. Alex, make sure everyone has a piece of chalk. Let's draw a picture of something from our Bible lesson today. If you want me to show your picture, I will. If you don't, that's alright."

Allister looked forward every other week to Sunday school. It wasn't so much that he didn't know the Bible stories Mother taught, since he'd learned them in the church and school in Quebec. But he enjoyed the way his mother taught, relating everything in the Bible to their life today.

A later Sunday school lesson from Genesis about twin brothers hit Allister the hardest. As his mother talked about chapter 27, Allister could see that when Jacob agreed to go along with a plan to deceive his father, a rift a mile wide grew between him and Esau, his twin brother. *Jim and I are close. Don't ever want that to happen to us. I must always be honest.*

Some evenings after he'd finished his homework, he read chapters in the Bible on his own. Two of his favourites were stories from the books of Jonah and Daniel. Allister loved to imagine being Jonah in the big fish, or Daniel in the den of lions. There were times, however, when he didn't understand what he read. Mother was always willing to explain words he didn't know, or the old-fashioned English phrases of the King James Bible he couldn't figure out. But there were times when even she wasn't able to satisfy his questions.

chapter eight

A Christmas Pageant

Once again during the weeks of early winter, Allister unhappily watched his father and older brothers hitch up their Clydesdales and shorthorns to both wagons on Sunday afternoons. They would be gone all week to work at Morton's sawmill on Turtle Mountain. With his father and brothers gone, Allister and Jim were in charge of barn chores before and after school.

On Saturdays, the menfolk returned with wagonloads of wood. One wagon supplied the cordwood for home, school, or sale in town, and the other was a load of lumber or shingles.

"Father, what are you going to do with all this lumber?" Allister asked, after watching the piles grow week by week.

"We need a shed next to the barn for our dump rake, reaper, and Mother's buggy."

"The rest of it and the piles of shingles," Will said, "are for my house on my homestead claim."

Allister figured that the best way he could help Will at this point was to manage the animal care, milking, barn cleaning, kindling splitting, and water hauling with only Jim's help. Allister knew that complaining would do little good, anyway. Jessie tried to take over the chicken care and egg gathering chores, since Mary was gone. But either Allister or Jim had to be on hand to monitor Jessie while she tried to do her chores. With their farm now boasting more livestock, Mother woke Allister and Jim every morning before dawn so that they had enough time to do everything before breakfast and school.

After school, there was little time for lingering. Chores took up most of the shortening daylight hours. Supper and homework happened after dark by lamplight.

Several times a week Mother bundled up Jessie, put her on the firewood skid, and pulled it to the schoolhouse. She timed her arrival for fifteen minutes before Mr. Webster usually left for his boarding place. From time to time, Allister noticed a change in his teacher's methods, material selections, or way of handling students. As time went on, Mr. Webster did less threatening and more frequent checking on his pupils while they worked on reading or arithmetic assignments. Allister noticed that he could spend less school time helping the other students and more on his own work. He was grateful that his mother took an interest in the teacher's progress as well his and Jim's.

Many afternoons after Mr. Webster had left the schoolhouse, strains of organ music bounced from the building across the snow around the barn and shed walls to Allister's ears as he worked in the barnyard. At supper one evening, he asked about some of the strange notes he'd heard.

"You're right, Allister. Most of the time, I practice the music we'll be singing during worship service or Sunday school. These days I'm practicing Christmas carols. The strange notes you hear are from Jessie. She likes to sit on the bench beside me and push the organ keys while I'm playing."

"Maybe Jessie has a musical ear," Jim suggested. "Could you teach her to play?"

Mother looked thoughtfully at her daughter. "Tried teaching her the alphabet and numbers. She has a very hard time with both. But music? It's worth a try, son."

———◆———

During a reading class one morning several weeks before Christmas, Mr. Webster handed out sheets of paper to Mabel, Allister, Jim, and Amy. "Read this play carefully. Start memorizing your parts. We'll practice this afternoon."

Allister studied his copy. In his mother's handwriting, the play told the Christmas story from the Bible. Jim was to be Joseph. Mabel was the angel Gabriel, Amy was Mary, and Allister was the narrator. There were parts for innkeepers, shepherds, an angelic chorus, bleating sheep, and a donkey, too. But the children who would play these parts needed to be taught their lines orally, since they were all beginners.

"Let's turn some desks around so we can practice our parts," Allister suggested.

In four desks facing each other in the back of the room, Allister, Mabel, Amy, and Jim read their parts. During their first read-through, Allister had fun putting in the animal sounds, such as the bleating of the sheep and the braying of the donkey. But as he saw how many lines the narrator had, Allister worried. *Didn't Mr. Webster say each of us is supposed to memorize our parts? How am I going to remember so many lines?*

That afternoon, Mr. Webster told all of Allister's schoolmates to put away their books and scribblers so that they could practice the play for the Christmas pageant. Pointing at the sheets of paper in his hand, he asked, "Mabel, you read the play this morning. Do you know when this story took place?"

She frowned and shook her head.

"The story of our play took place almost two thousand years ago," Mr. Webster said. "Georgie, that's a long time ago, isn't it? Even before your great-great-grandfather's time. Does anyone know where the story took place? Was it here in Canada?"

Allister and the other students who had read the play shook their heads. The younger students shrugged.

"Alright, where?"

Allister raised his hand.

"Yes, Allister?"

"Was it in Israel?"

"Yes, that's right," Mr. Webster said. "Where is that country on this world map?"

Allister searched the entire outline of countries. Finally, he said, "There is no Israel on the map, Mr. Webster."

"You're right. Today, in 1893, there is no Israel. Bigger, stronger nations took the land and scattered its people, but two thousand years ago it was here," the teacher said, pointing at a spot east of the Mediterranean Sea. "In our play, an Israeli girl is engaged to a young man. Amy, what is the girl's name?"

"Mary."

"Jim, what is the young man's name?"

"Joseph."

"Mabel, an angel comes to Mary to give her a special message from God. What is the angel's name?"

"Gabriel."

"That's right. Mary, you stand there," the teacher said, pointing to the window next to the organ. "Gabriel, you stand up on the organ bench."

Amy took her place. Mabel climbed onto the bench.

"Narrator, you stand up here." The teacher pointed to the spot right behind the podium that he had just set on his desk. "Speak up when it's your turn to say your piece. Now begin."

Everything went along well until it was time for all the other children to learn their parts. Bedlam broke out as each group or child practiced their lines. "Baa, baa ... I'm sorry, there's no... Baa, baa, baa ... Glory to God in the highest and ... Hee haw, hee haw ... Let's go to Bethlehem ..."

Mr. Webster put his hands over his ears. "Stop!" he yelled.

When everyone was quiet, he had each child or group of children practice the parts, one at a time.

Allister groaned as each of the younger students stumbled through their parts. *Will everyone remember their lines when it is time for the Christmas pageant? How will I? I don't think I can remember every word the narrator is supposed to say.* Allister felt his stomach tighten into a knot.

Most afternoons after that, Allister and the rest of the students at Wood Lake School practiced the play. Allister did his best to memorize the narrator's speeches. With Jim's help, Allister practiced after school in the barn while they did chores. He enlisted Mabel's help during recesses and noon breaks. It became harder and harder for Allister to eat anything. The knot in his stomach grew and grew.

During one noon break ten days before the pageant, Mother asked, "Allister, what's wrong with you? Are you sick? You're hardly eating any of your dinner."

Allister rubbed his stomach. "I'm just so nervous. I'm doing my best, but I don't think I can memorize all of my part for the Christmas pageant."

"What part is that?"

"The narrator."

Mother gasped. "Who told you that you had to memorize all of those lines?"

"Mr. Webster. He said everyone was supposed to memorize their part in the play."

"But that's pages and pages." Mother frowned. "The one person who should be allowed to read his lines is the narrator. That way when one of the other students can't remember his or her piece, the narrator has the information right in front of him and can cue those who forget their lines. I'll talk to your teacher today after school. Relax, Allister, and eat your dinner."

Allister let out his anxiety with a whoosh. *Saved by Mother. Still, I have to say many lines in front of all those parents. And be responsible to cue everyone else? Not a picnic. I think I'd rather do ten pages of arithmetic or four hours of haying.*

Several afternoons the week before the pageant, Mother came at 2:30 to help all the children learn some Christmas songs. She enlisted Caroline's help to make some simple costumes, including one set of donkey ears and three pairs of sheep ears. On the two afternoons before the school's Christmas pageant, both women were on hand to help with dress rehearsals.

The Friday evening before Christmas, the one-room schoolhouse filled with the children and their families for the first-ever Wood Lake School Christmas pageant. Half a dozen fathers brought lanterns and hung them from the roof beams. Mother and Caroline got all the children into their costumes.

Just as Mr. Webster walked towards the platform to start the performance, little Georgie jumped up from the floor where he'd been sitting "I gotta go!" he yelled.

Laughter rippled through the audience.

"Alright," Mr. Webster said. "Hurry back."

Georgie ran out the door. Allister watched him through the window. The little boy stopped short of the outhouse and stood there.

I wonder what's wrong, Allister thought. Running outside, Allister asked, "Georgie, what's the matter?"

"I'm scared. It's dark in there."

"I know. I'll go in there with you. You'll be alright."

Georgie put his hand in Allister's, and the two boys entered the outhouse together.

After they returned to the schoolhouse, their teacher lined up all twelve first grade students for the opening song.

"Jingle bells, jingle bells …" piped the children while Jim stood behind them shaking a strap of their harness bells as Mother played the organ.

Then it was time for their play. After Mr. Webster introduced it, Allister stood behind the teacher's desk. Gabriel climbed onto the organ bench. Mary stood next to the window, facing the audience and the angel. "Hail, you that are highly favoured, the Lord is with you; blessed are you among women," Gabriel began.

Everything went as practiced until Allister narrated, "And there were in the same country shepherds abiding in the field, keeping watch over their flock by night."

As he spoke his lines, three sheep and their shepherds got up on the platform. The sheep milled about, baaing. The main shepherd put her finger to her lips and loudly said, "Sh!" The sheep paid no attention and continued to mill about and baa. The angels climbed up on the teacher's desk. Mabel, who was the main angel, hollered at the milling sheep, "It is night time, sheep. Go to sleep!"

Several of the children giggled and all became quiet. The sheep lay down on the straw.

"And lo, the angel of the Lord came upon them, the glory of the Lord shone round about them, and they were sore afraid," Allister narrated.

The shepherds crouched as if afraid, looking up at the angels standing on the teacher's desk.

"Don't be afraid," the main angel said. "For, see, I bring you good tidings of great joy, which shall be to all people. For unto you is born this day in the city of David a Saviour, which is Christ the Lord. And this shall be a sign to you: you shall find the babe wrapped in swaddling clothes, lying in a manger."

Then all the angels said together, "Glory to God in the highest, and on earth peace, good will towards men."

Mother struck a chord to start the shepherds' song. At first Etta was the only one singing, "Angels we have heard on high, sweetly singing o'er the plains …" Eventually the other shepherds remembered the song and joined her. Then together the angels sang the chorus of the song in two-part harmony: "Gloria in excelsis Deo, Gloria in excelsis Deo."

As the angels climbed off the teacher's desk and threaded their way to the back of the room, a smattering of applause rippled through the audience.

"Let's now go to Bethlehem," the main shepherd said to the others. The sheep got off the platform and sat down on the floor nearby. Etta led the shepherds towards the back of the room.

Whew! Allister let out a deep breath. *Everyone is remembering their lines and what they're supposed to do. We just might make it through this play without any more problems.*

Mary followed the "donkey" to the platform, and Joseph placed the manger in front of her. Taking the swaddled baby from his mother, who was sitting in the front row, Joseph put him back in the hay. Objecting to being put down, the baby started to howl.

Oh, no, Allister thought. *Now what should I do?* He looked at the baby's mother. She nodded and motioned for Jim to pick up and rock the wailing infant. Joseph took her cue. After a minute of fussing, the baby "Jesus" quieted.

Relieved that one more disaster had been dodged, Allister completed his narration. "And they came with haste and found Mary and Joseph and the babe lying in a manger."

After the shepherds had gathered around Mary and Joseph, Allister announced the end of their play.

Mr. Webster, Mother, Caroline, and all the Wood Lake School children lined up on the platform. At the teacher's cue, everyone bowed.

As the families clapped, Allister heard a loud, "Ho, ho, ho!" Everyone turned to·see a big man wearing a fake white beard come into the room through the schoolhouse door. "Merry Christmas, everyone! Ho, ho, ho, ho!" he shouted. "Are there any good boys and girls here?"

Hands flew up among the school children.

"Me, Santa! Over here. And I've been good all year!" It was Georgie. He was practically jumping up and down.

Through the laughing, clapping people, Santa made his way towards the children up front. The little brothers and sisters of the school-age children wiggled out of their parents' arms to join the fun. Santa swung the big sack he was carrying onto the teacher's desk. One by one, all the children received a small package tied up with string.

When Allister reached for his, Santa winked at him. *I'm not sure, but I think Santa looks a little like my brother, John, stuffed with a goose down pillow or two.* Allister laughed. *I wonder if Jessie knows who this Santa really is.* Seeing the delight on her face when Santa gave her a present, Allister decided not to spoil her fun.

Parents gathered around the teacher and his helpers to shake their hands and thank them for their work with their children. "See you at the Christmas Eve service," the families called to each other as they stepped into their stone boats and sleighs. Wooden and steel runners shushed through snow, carrying in every direction from the schoolhouse the sounds of excited children.

The McRuer family, the teacher, and several others stayed to tidy up, sweep the floor, and blow out the lanterns.

"Caroline, Etta, climb in," Mr. McRuer said. "I'll give you a ride home."

"Students, see you the first Monday of February," the teacher said as he locked the schoolhouse door. "Merry Christmas and Happy New Year, everyone!"

By the time Allister walked home with his brothers, he had figured out that their Christmas vacation was going to be much longer than the ones they had in Quebec.

After Mr. McRuer returned from dropping off their neighbours, Allister asked, "Father, why is our Christmas vacation almost six weeks long?"

"January on the Manitoba prairies is bitterly cold. Its wild winds and deep snow can be deadly for small children without enough warm clothing. Many of your schoolmates have to walk several miles to get to our schoolhouse. The school board thought everyone would be safer at home during the worst of it."

"Won't that make it harder for us to finish all our studies for the year?"

"School runs through the end of June. That should be time enough."

Hmm. Through the end of June? Allister smiled. *If I'm at school, I'll miss out on some of the planting and weeding. Alright by me!*

chapter nine

One Wild Ride

Two days before Christmas, as Allister walked back to the house from the barn, he heard steel pinging on steel on the other side of the lumber pile. Curious, he stuck his head around the corner of the pile. Against the stack of lumber leaned the wheels of Mother's buggy. Its detached canopy rested in the snow nearby. Mr. McRuer was working on the bottom of the buggy's body that lay upside down. *What in the world is father doing to mother's buggy?* When his father caught Allister spying on him, he paused in his work. "Come hold this, son."

"Father, I didn't know you could turn a buggy into a sleigh."

"Neither did I, until I saw these attachments advertised in a catalogue at Desford's general store."

"Mother will be delighted. She hates to be house-bound during Manitoba's winters."

"Don't tell her about these runners. They're her Christmas present."

"Alright. I won't."

Christmas Eve morning, the scents of fresh pine and roasting beef filled the house from cellar to roof beams. A Christmas tree with a popcorn and cranberry garland took up a corner of the sitting room once again. A loaf of dark-brown, fragrant fruitcake rested ready on the dining room table. A bowl of Mother's plum pudding sat in its hot water bath, steaming to perfection on the stove in the kitchen. After she put the finishing touches on her potato casserole and slid it into the oven, she set Allister and Jim to work. "Boys, I need you to split more kindling, and fill these large pots with snow. Bath time this afternoon. Christmas Eve service is this evening. But first, get several jars of corn and a couple of pounds of carrots from the cellar."

Later when he left the house to chop the wood, Allister saw John and Dan disappear behind the lumber piles, carrying shovels. *What are they up to now?*

———

After their delicious Christmas Eve day dinner, Mother invited Jessie and the twins into the sitting room. She handed each of them a heavy object wrapped in burlap and tied with a string. "Time to open your one Christmas Eve gift."

When Allister untied the string, his shiny metal gift puzzled him.

"It's an ice skate," Mother said. "You clamp it to the bottom of your boots and skate on the ice."

"What ice?"

"The pond behind the lumber piles."

"But that pond is covered with two feet of sn ... oh." Allister remembered his brothers and their shovels. "But Mother, don't I need two skates, one for each boot?"

"Yes, Allister, you're right," Mother said. "Didn't have the money to buy two pairs of skates. Sorry, boys. You'll have to take turns."

Allister nodded, but thought, *Jim probably doesn't mind, but I do.*

Jessie's present wasn't a skate. It was a small wooden cradle.

"The little bed is for Missy," Jim said. "Jessie, go get your doll."

Jumping up, Jessie clambered up the stairs to her room. When she returned with Missy, Jim set the doll in the small bed and pushed its side up and down. "See. You can rock your baby to sleep."

Jessie clapped her hands. "Jimmie, me try." She sat on the floor and beamed as she rocked Missy.

"Come on, Jim. Let's try our skates," Allister said.

"Alright, but I'm first."

"Why do you have to be first?" Allister demanded, his temper rising.

"Boys," Mother interrupted, "no fighting. Jim, you're first. Then after a short try, give Allister the skates."

"Yes, Mother," Allister and Jim chimed together. Reluctantly, Allister handed his brother his skate.

Sitting on the bench by the back door, Jim removed his boots and tried to adjust the clamps to fit the soles.

Just then, John came in. "Put your boots back on, Jim. I'll attach the skates for you."

With the pair of blades under him, Jim stood on wobbly legs. Attempting a step, he fell flat on his face. One of his ankles had buckled.

"Here, old man, hold onto this," John said, handing Jim an upside-down broom.

Allister snickered.

"You think this is easy? We'll see when it's your turn!" Jim retorted.

After bundling up, the three of them went to the pond. John walked backwards onto the ice, holding onto Jim's hands. Jim tried walking on his skates on the ice; only his grip on John's hands kept him on his feet.

"I've never been skating myself," John said, "but I've seen skaters push their feet sideways. That seemed to propel them forward."

Jim tried it and moved forward without John holding him. Not knowing how to stop, however, the "skater" dove into the snow bank on the opposite end of the pond. John plucked his brother out of the bank and turned him around. Jim zipped to the other side and laughed as he fell once again into a bank.

"My turn now," Allister hollered, thinking, *That looks like fun.*

"Alright," John said. "You two can just trade boots, since you wear the same size shoes."

Putting on his twin's boot-skates, Allister grabbed John's hands and copied what he had seen Jim do. John let go. With the snow bank on the opposite end approaching fast, Allister twisted his feet to the left. As his body hurtled after his feet, he leaned into the turn to keep his balance.

"Gee! How did you do that?" Jim whistled.

Allister's turn headed him back the way he had just come. Still not knowing how to stop, he tried leaning back. Whoosh! His feet flew from under him. Thump! *Ow. That wasn't fun.* Groaning, he rolled over onto his hands and knees and crawled to the nearest snow bank.

"You alright?" John asked. "Here, let me help you up."

"Man, that ice is hard! I don't think ..."

"Try it again," John interrupted. "Remember what Father said about riding horses?"

"If a horse throws you, get back on right away," Jim announced. "He said that if you don't, you'll always be afraid of horses."

"Right! This is like learning to ride a horse. Get up. Try again," John said. "This time don't lean back. A snow bank makes a whole lot softer landing than the ice."

Allister did try several more times, but he didn't get as much of a thrill out of skating as his twin seemed to.

Late that evening as the Christmas Eve service began in the schoolhouse, Joe and Mary slid onto the front bench next to Father. From the pump organ, Mother led the gathering of families in Christmas carols. When it was their turn, all of the children from Mother's Sunday school class, including Jessie, stepped onto the front platform and sang "Away in a Manger." Allister's classmate, Mabel, sang a duet with her mother, "Angels We Have Heard on High."

Since Allister wasn't doing any of the Old and New Testament readings this time, he could relax and really listen. He marvelled at the detail in the Old Testament reading from Micah. Micah told exactly which Israeli town Jesus was going to be born in—Bethlehem. *I thought Mother told me that Micah wrote his book hundreds of years before Jesus was born. How did Micah know?*

While Allister pondered his question, Reverend Forsythe lit a candle and touched its flame to Mother's. She moved to light Joe's, and the flame moved from candle to candle among the parents of all the families. When all the candles were lit, the pastor led his flock outside, where everyone stood for a few moments in the starlit cold to sing one more carol.

"O little town of Bethlehem, how still we see thee lie! Above thy deep and dreamless sleep ..."

Snuffing out their candles and wishing each other "Merry Christmas," families hurried home to escape the frosty fingers of Manitoba's deepening chill. Before the McRuer family walked home, they blew out the lanterns, closed off the fire in the barrel stove, and locked the door. Joe pulled Jessie on the firewood skid at a trot, stomping and snorting, pretending to be Shalazar. The little girl's laughter rippled across the snow. Mother and Mary followed Father, walking arm in arm and chatting. Allister kicked at snow clumps as he went. He was glad Mary and Joe would be staying with them for a few days. He was doubly glad that unlike last year's miles of a chilly ride in a stone boat, this year's trip home from their Christmas Eve service was a half mile walk.

———◆———

On Christmas morning, the brightness of the sunlight fooled Allister. Snow underfoot to the outhouse gave off a crisp crunch. *Not a warm day at all*, he thought.

After chores and breakfast, everyone gathered in the sitting room for the Christmas gifts. Allister was grateful to unwrap his—a pair of pants and a winter coat. He was fairly sure both garments were cut down versions of John's old ones. Since Mother was quite a seamstress, no one outside of the family could ever tell they weren't new. When Jim held up his "new" garments, Allister guessed that they had once been Will's. Allister appreciated his mother's thoughtfulness. She had sized John's clothes for him, not Will's. Will was less likely to give Jim trouble about wearing his hand-me-downs.

When Jim helped Jessie untie her gift, Allister saw that Mother had done the same thing for his little sister. Cutting down an old coat of Mary's, Mother had created a "new" coat for Jessie and another little one just like it. Excited, Jessie put on her coat and the tiny coat on Missy. "Twins," she said, pointing at her doll and herself.

"Mother, your gift is outside," Father said. "But first we need to blindfold you to keep it a surprise."

Mother put on her coat and hat, and Will tied a folded dishtowel over her eyes. While Father and Will guided Mother out the front door, Allister ran into the kitchen to grab his cap and mittens from the pockets of his old coat near the back door. Scooting back into the sitting room, he quickly pulled on his new coat before joining the family outside.

John led Shalazar hitched to the buggy-now-sleigh into the front yard. Pointing at the seat in the sleigh, he said, "Allister, get up here."

Scrambling in, Allister took the reins from John. Gripping them as firmly as he could, Allister waited for his mother to get in the sleigh.

Father removed the blindfold from Mother's eyes. "Merry Christmas!"

"Mother, now you have a way to visit Mary anytime," Joe said.

"Oh, oh, oh, oh!" Mother exclaimed, "Oh, my dear husband! Thank you!" Mother wrapped her arms around Father, repeatedly kissing his cheek.

Then she held him out by his elbows at arms' length. "Where did you get money for a sleigh?" she asked, mockingly fierce.

"I didn't," Father said, grinning. "It's your buggy on runners!"

"You clever, clever man!"

With John's help, Mother got into the sleigh. She laughed, clapping her hands as if delighted.

Shalazar took that sound as the signal to fly down the lane. It was a good thing that Allister had already braced his feet against the front board of the sleigh and wrapped the reins around his hands. Now he fought the horse with all his might for control. *Clunk!* Shalazar took the bit in his back teeth and ran at will. Allister strained at the reins, but with the bit in his teeth, the horse could ignore any backward pull.

Allister heard his father holler, "Turn Shalazar's head. Put both hands on one rein and pull hard."

As they approached the road, Allister hauled on the left rein with both hands, just like his father had told him, and managed to turn the galloping horse's head. Shalazar followed his head left, turning onto the road. *Whew! At least we aren't careening across open fields. But Shalazar hasn't slowed down even a little.*

As they rounded the corner, Allister felt the sleigh slip sideways over the snow. He was too scared to think the whoosh around the corner thrilling. Allister glanced at Mother. She was gripping the side of the sleigh, her lips pressed tight. Her face and the back of her hands were as pale as snow.

Shalazar tore down the road, past the schoolhouse, and raced towards Desford, the small town more than four miles from their homestead.

Maybe someone in town can help stop this horse, Allister thought. *But who will be out and about on such a bitterly cold Christmas Day. And why hasn't this horse wound down any?*

In the blink of an eye, they swept through the silent town. There was no use yelling. No one appeared at the sound of Shalazar's mad dash. The horse raced on.

The turnoff for the town of Cherry Creek was the next danger. *At the speed Shalazar is going, can he make the turn without overturning the sleigh?* Allister worried.

A quarter of a mile before they reached the turnoff, Allister saw a wide flat area to the right of their westward road. It had no bushes, fences, ravines, or slopes to cause trouble. *My arms are getting so tired, but if I could just turn Shalazar in a wide circle, I might be able to stop him.* Allister hollered, "Mother, please help me. Let's pull him around to the right."

His mother let go of the side of the sleigh and put her hands over Allister's. The two of them forcefully arched the plunging animal's head to the right. Gradually curving in a wide circle off the road and into deep snow took the wind out of Shalazar's sailing strides. By the second turn around the circle, he was puffing. He slowed to a trot. At the end of the third time around, he stopped, sides heaving.

"Out of breath, are you, you menace?" Allister shouted. "Serves you right!"

Allister felt Shalazar release the bit from his back teeth and yield to the pressure of the reins on his mouth. Turning the horse in a tighter circle and back onto the road east, Allister held Shalazar to a trot. The return trip through Desford went without incident.

East of town, Joe met them on Jake. This time, Shalazar stopped when Allister pulled back on the reins.

"Good job, Allister. Looks like you have him under control now."

"Well, I had some help from Mother," he said, smiling at her.

"How far did the rascal take you?" Joe asked, studying the willful horse, his frothy mouth and lathered, heaving sides.

"Almost to the Cherry Creek turnoff."

Joe whistled. Turning to Mother, Joe asked, "Annie, are you alright?"

"I am now," she said with a wan smile.

After they got back to the farmyard, Allister turned the horse and sleigh over to Father and Jim. When he entered the warmth of the kitchen, Allister realized his teeth were doing their own dance. Mary took one look at her mother and brother and worried out loud about frostbite. Wrapping the returnees in blankets and placing chairs for them close to the stove, Mary brought in handfuls of snow to rub on their foreheads, cheeks, and the backs of Mother's hands.

It took a great while to warm up. The numbness was followed by pain. It felt like a thousand pins and needles poking into skin that had been exposed to such a long chill from their frightful ride over miles of snow through whipping wind.

While Mother and Allister were thawing out, John grilled him with a dozen questions. Thumping his younger brother heartily on the back, John added, "Allister, you did very well. Be proud of yourself. You saved your mother's life as well as your own. Don't worry, Joe and I'll fix it so that horse can never take the bit in his teeth again!"

Every day for the next several days, Allister saw Joe hitch Shalazar to the sleigh. Fastening a leather strap to the bit under the horse's jaw, John tightened it so that the bit could only sit in the space in the horse's mouth between his front and back teeth. He would never be able to clamp the bit in his teeth and ignore his driver again. Then, lashing the horse with the knotted end of a rope, the men pushed him into a gallop down the road. An hour or so later, Shalazar returned, sweaty and with sides heaving. Each time, he came back at a more reasonable pace with his head a little lower. After unhitching him, Jim always walked the horse to cool him slowly.

"Mother, I think Shalazar will behave for you now," John said several days later.

"Certainly hope so," she said. "One wild ride is more than enough!"

While Joe and John worked on Shalazar, Father and Dan butchered the last of the young Angus. Although its meat would freeze and keep in Manitoba's winter weather for some time, there was always a chance that the lingering scent of a kill might attract wolves from Turtle Mountain.

For that reason, Mother and Mary, with Allister's and Jim's help, put most of the meat into canning jars for storage in the cellar.

When it was time for Mary and Joe to return home, they took some jars of the canned beef with them. Since a fox had stolen one of their chickens, Mother promised a replacement from her flock in the spring. It was too cold to take a chicken out of its warm pen in the barn during the dead of winter.

Not many days after Mary and Joe left, Will returned from the sawmill. He had gone back to work after the Christmas holiday only to discover that the mill had temporarily suspended operations. He was to return to the mill in a month if the weather permitted.

The deep cold froze the McRuers' cistern and the well water in their pump house. The entire family hunkered down to wait out the bitter winter weather. Keeping everyone and every animal alive turned into a full-time job.

Allister didn't relish the constant hauling of pots of melted snow out to the barn. Getting warm enough water out to their chickens was especially difficult. In spite of his and Jim's efforts, two of Mother's chickens died from the cold.

chapter ten

Captives of a White Out

A llister was sometimes amazed at what the prairie wind could do with even a small covering of snow. One morning he and Jim came out of the barn after chores to face a wall of swirling, howling white. The house had disappeared! In fact, Allister couldn't see any other farm building. "Oh boy! This time we have no guide rope between buildings to hang onto. Today's storm must be so sudden that even Father and John weren't aware it was coming."

With a grunt, Jim pulled his neck scarf over his nose and mouth and stepped out into the blizzard. Allister grabbed Jim by the back of his coat and hollered to be heard above the roar of the wind. "Where are you going?"

"If I go straight out from the barn twenty feet, maybe I can see the house," Jim shouted over his shoulder.

"No, Jim." Allister yelled, keeping his grip on his brother's coat. "You get that far from the barn, and you won't be able to see either building."

Jim shuffled backward a few steps.

Allister continued to cling to Jim. "You do remember the stories we've heard of people wandering on this wide open prairie in a white out and being found later miles from their farms and frozen to death, don't you? We'd better not leave the barn until it blows over."

Allister let go when Jim returned to the barn. Standing in the doorway, he stared at the wall of snow roaring past him. "How long do you think that'll take?" he grumped.

"Who knows? Could be days!"

"Maybe we'll end up like Mother's two chickens."

"Don't say things like that!"

The twins went back inside the barn and shut the door.

"Let's make ourselves a straw cave," Allister suggested.

The boys gathered and piled up straw in the centre of the barn. They spent the next couple of hours curled up in their cave, sitting or lying back to back.

"I'm thirsty," Allister said.

"Yep, me too. Could drink from the cattle trough or horses' buckets."

"No thank you. Fresh snow sounds better."

"Alright by me!"

Taking turns, they went out with a rope tied around their waists to get fresh snow to eat whenever they got thirsty.

Noon and their normal dinner time slipped by. Allister felt his stomach complain about being empty. Jim's tummy growled too. "I heard that," Allister said.

They both laughed.

Jim got up and cracked the barn door open to see if the storm had let up. "Still howling. I'm hungry! Too many days of this, and a growling stomach won't seem so funny."

"Wish Father or John would come looking for us."

As the light coming in the window turned from white to gray, Allister could feel the temperature dropping inside the barn, in spite of all the animals giving off heat. He checked the horses' buckets. A skim of ice was gradually growing on the surface of the water in them. To keep warm, Allister and Jim curled up in their straw cave, pressing against each other's warm back. They drifted off to sleep.

In his dreams, Allister heard someone calling his name and felt a firm hand shake his shoulder. Waking up with a start, he opened his eyes to see Father's anxious face peering into his. "Are you alright, son?"

"Yes, Father." Allister got up. His limbs felt stiff from the cold. He stretched and wiggled his hands and feet to get some life back into them.

"Smart lads. Didn't leave the barn when you couldn't see the house."

"We were afraid you had left the barn and gotten lost in the storm," John said.

Jim grimaced as he stood and copied Allister's movements. "How did you get out here?"

"Father tied a rope around my waist and fastened the other end to the metal ring next to the back door."

"John and I held onto each other to fight against the wind," Will said. "We moved from side to side at this end of the rope until we stumbled against the barn."

"Once they signaled that they had tied their end of the rope to the ring by the barn door, Dan and I could come out too," Father said. "Your disappearance really frightened Mother and Jessie. Better get back in the house."

"Go ahead," John said. "We'll do the chores."

"When you didn't return from chores this morning, we tried calling you from the back door," Dan said. "Mother even stood for a while outside with her back against the wall of the house, banging on one of her pots."

"Sorry. We couldn't hear a thing," Jim said, shaking his head. "The wind was howling so loud!"

"I'll walk in front of you two until you get in," Dan offered. "Don't let go of the rope."

Allister had no desire to go out into the still raging storm, because he was thoroughly chilled. But his father and older brothers had already risked a lot to come looking for him and Jim. The thought of a warm spot by Mother's stove and the hot meal she would probably have ready for him helped Allister move towards the barn door and the blizzard outside. *Besides, Mother won't be content until she has laid eyes on us.*

True to his word, Dan took the lead. His large frame acted as a welcome windbreak. Jim and Allister followed close behind, hanging onto the guide rope as if their lives depended on it. Facing into the blast forced Allister to tug his coat collar across his face. His breaths came in painful gasps from the icy air. Once they were safely inside the house, Dan turned around and headed back along the rope, stumbling through the drifts as the wind tried to knock him off his feet.

Just inside the back door, the twins found themselves smothered in a Mother and Jessie hug. "Oh, I am so glad they found you," Mother said.

"Where were you?" Jessie peered up at her brothers. "You scared us."

"In the barn, out of this awful wind, Jessie." Jim knelt in front of his sister. "I'm alright. See!" He took off his mittens and held her hands between his.

"Oh, you cold!" Jessie frowned and pulled away.

Allister moved towards the stove, pulled off his mittens, and held his hands close to the stove's toasty surface. "Mother, we didn't leave the barn when we couldn't see the house. We stayed there in a big pile of straw."

"You boys must be famished." Mother poured and handed them cups of hot tea. "Start with these. They'll warm you up."

After their ordeal in the barn, Allister was grateful that other members of the family were doing the chores and chopping the kindling.

As the wind howled its way through January, and the snow piled up against the walls of their farm buildings, Allister kept a promise he had made to himself. While Father and his older brothers used any spare hours to work on harness and equipment repairs, he studied. He talked Jim into joining his steady march through their reading, math, spelling, handwriting, geography, and history homework.

One morning while Allister and Jim were bent over their books on the dining room table, their father came and stood behind Allister. "What are you boys doing? You'd better come out into the kitchen and work with John or me to learn about harness repair. After all, that skill will be something you'll need to have when you're farming your own claim."

Allister turned to face his father. "Please, Father, let us do our schoolwork. We have a lot of catching up to do."

"Catching up?" Father frowned.

"Yes, Father," Allister continued his plea. "When school opened last fall, we had to complete the sixth grade work we missed because we left the school in Quebec a couple of months early the spring of 1892 to be out here to help with planting. Remember?"

Father nodded. "But, son, you will need ..."

Allister wasn't finished with his plea. "Father, after waiting a whole year for a school to go to, Jim and I lost two more weeks of our studies at the beginning of this school year to help with harvest. Being pulled out of class for so many months makes me feel that we're really behind in our seventh grade subjects."

Father sighed. "Alright, son. Stick to your studies for now. There will be time for you to learn these other skills later."

Relieved, Allister dove back into his studies immediately. Jim, however, sat and watched his father and older brother for a few minutes before returning to his books.

As the twins worked on their reading book, Allister could see that all the reading done the previous year had really helped him. Jim often complained that their schoolwork seemed like the white-out they had faced from their barn door. Attempts to help his brother with the more difficult vocabulary taxed not only Allister's own word knowledge, but also his patience and ability to act as Jim's tutor.

Mother was no longer able to bail them out. Her own education had ended at sixth grade, and Father's at fourth. Although his older brothers had completed Grade 8, they either couldn't remember enough to explain anything or, worse yet, hadn't understood their schoolwork in the first place.

Even if no one in his family could help him, scrambling on top of the "snow bank" of knowledge was definitely Allister's goal. He desperately clung to his hope for more education. *So what if no one else in my family has done it? Does that mean I shouldn't or can't? I'll show them all I can!*

Allister was most relieved when school resumed. At times, Mr. Webster still assigned work without enough explanation or instruction. At the risk of being thought a pest, he followed his teacher to his desk to ask additional questions. When Mr. Webster was too busy with the other students, Allister bothered Wood Lake School's only eighth grade student, Mabel, for some help. To pay her back for her time, Allister helped her study for tests. In the end, that helped Allister, too. By helping Mabel, he was learning what kinds of information an eighth grader had to know.

Among his favourite subjects was geography. When Mr. Webster assigned the drawing of a map of North America that spring, Allister begged Mother for a couple of large pieces of paper. He spent hours poring over the school's atlas and drawing every coastline, river, mountain, lake, province, state, and city as perfectly as he could. With his very best handwriting, he labelled everything.

When he finished the map, Mother admired it greatly. "My, that map is a work of art, Allister!"

Jim did the same assignment, of course. But his understanding of map construction meant "put the required items somewhere in a continent's outline." In Jim's mind, it was far more important to learn the "geography" of a horse. He spent hours grooming and training Maggie's colt.

Putting horses ahead of homework? Allister pondered Jim's choice. *A big mistake?*

chapter eleven

Spring Break Up

With the arrival of March came Will's final preparation for his departure to his homestead claim. All three older brothers had been busy making furniture for Will's place: a coat rack, a cupboard, a table, and a couple of chairs. Father had sold two additional stone boat loads of wheat at Desford and ordered a small cook stove and a keg of nails for Will to take with him. As Allister watched the accumulation of supplies for his older brother's farm, he couldn't help being thrilled that his tormenter would soon be gone.

One Friday morning at breakfast, Will announced: "Winter isn't quite over. Snow still on the ground. The Pembina River a solid block of ice. But that's one reason to go now. Make that river crossing easier. So if the weather's good, I want to leave tomorrow."

"Alright, son." Mr. McRuer set down his cup of tea. "Good thing you wintered over here. This last one would have been deadly for you on the open prairie."

John nodded. "That's for sure."

"Angus and Dan can go with you," Father offered, "and help you get started."

For the first time in months, Allister saw Will smile. "Didn't expect any help, but thank you, that'd be great."

A cloudless sky crowned Saturday. After breakfast, Allister joined the rest of the family in helping Will finish the loading of the wagons. On top of the one with lumber and shingles, they stacked and tied Will's wood furniture, the packing crates of his clothes and personal items, and the bed and bedding he had been using at home. On top of the other one with the lumber and poles, they loaded a tarpaulin for a tent, the sacks of feed and seed that Father gave him, and numerous farming and building tools, including Will's walking plow.

Before the three brothers finished their loading, Mother handed the twins many items to tuck into the loads. There was a crate with bars of soap, towels, and kitchen items. Another crate had food supplies. On top, Mother had wrapped up several loaves of her fresh-baked bread.

Allister smiled. In spite of his resentment of his nemesis' constant teasing, he was glad to see his family supply Will with everything he would need to survive on the prairie out on his own. *At least my brother won't starve.*

At the last minute, Mother handed Jim an empty jug to fill with fresh drinking water since they had finally managed to thaw out the pump under the windmill that had frozen solid during the worst of the winter's deep chill. Jim handed Will the full jug of water to put in the wagon he would be driving.

Mother wrapped her arms around the son she would probably not see for a very long time. "I know you're anxious to make a life of your own, but I love you and I'm going to miss you. Remember you are always welcome to come home for a visit."

Allister looked down to see Jessie grab Will around his legs. She looked up at her brother. "I love you. Be nice to people. Then they love you too."

Will smiled at Jessie and patted her head. Turning to Jim, he shook hands. "Be sure to help Father."

At the very last, Will turned to Allister and offered his hand. "Goodbye, student. See you in April."

Only a small dig this time. Allister felt relieved. *April? What was happening in April?*

When Mr. McRuer came out of the barn leading Maggie's foal, Will went to say goodbye. Father and son shook hands. Before Will could turn to walk away, Father handed Will the colt's lead rope. "He's yours, son. Take good care of him. Jim has him well started."

Will gulped and mumbled, "Thank you, Father." With a look of disbelief at his father's unexpected generosity, Will tied the young horse to the back of the wagon.

Allister glanced at Jim, half expecting to see a frown. But Jim was smiling. Allister wondered if Jim had known all along their father planned to give Maggie's colt to Will.

"Hup! Hup!" At the gentle prod of Will's stick, the shorthorns moved down the lane.

Dan and John slapped the reins on their team's backs, and Jake and Maggie followed Will's wagon. Part way down the lane, the colt whinnied and tried to pull free. Seeing his mother right behind him, he calmed down and moved along.

While Allister watched them go, he thought about the hole Will would leave. As delighted as Allister felt about the family bully moving to the "other side of the moon," he knew everyone else, especially his father, would miss Will. He could do the work of a full grown man. Allister knew he and Jim couldn't make up the difference ... at least not yet. Allister worried. *Will Father expect more of us?*

———◆———

Calf watch began before the return of John and Dan. Although Father did most of it, Jim and Allister did their share before and after school. This season, they had five Angus cows and Bessie to monitor. They kept the closest tabs on their milk cow. She'd been bred to their Angus bull, a much bigger animal than any Guernsey bull. Hopefully she'd have no trouble with the delivery of her larger-than-normal baby.

In the pitch dark of the second week of calf watch, Allister felt Father shaking him awake. "Wake up Jim. Get down to the barn as soon as you both can."

In minutes, Jim and Allister were dressed and standing in the cattle pen inside the barn. They rubbed the sleep out of their eyes and tried to figure out what was going on. Bessie lay on her side, grunting and rolling her eyes.

"She's been like this for hours," Father said. "We need to get that calf out of her now, if we can. Allister, here's a clean bucket. Come back with warm water from the stove, a bar of soap, and several towels."

Running back into the house, Allister filled the bucket with water from the big pot Mother kept heating on the back of the stove. When Allister returned with all the items, Jim plunged his right arm into the bucket and scrubbed and rinsed it up to his armpit. The boy's shirt lay in the straw.

"Now, son, lay down behind her and push your right arm inside the cow. Tell me what part of the calf you feel."

Allister watched in amazement.

"A tail. Hind end."

"Oh, that's why she's having trouble. Gotta turn the calf around, if you can. Feel for its head and front legs."

Jim pushed his right arm in further, almost up to his neck. "Got it."

"Grab a leg and pull towards you."

The cow, feeling the calf turning inside her, started to get up.

"Allister, sit on her head," Father said. "Don't let her get up."

For about five minutes, Jim struggled to turn the calf's head into position. "It's there now."

"Alright, son, back away from her."

Jim pulled out his arm and stood up. The top part of his body, his face, and even his hair were covered with flecks of bloody slime. "Oh my!" he exclaimed through chattering teeth. "The inside of that cow was nice and warm. Out here, I'm freezing."

"I'll hold Bessie's head down, Allister. Help your brother wash and dry himself off. He's cold because he's wet."

Ripping a towel in half, Allister helped Jim wipe clean. Handing Jim one of the towels, Allister used a second to dry off his brother's hair and back. Soon Jim was sitting in the straw, clean and dry with his shirt on.

"Come on, Bessie." Father stroked the cow's neck. "Shouldn't be so hard now."

Allister watched a series of contractions ripple along the cow's body. A red head appeared. Front legs came, and then a red and white body was followed by more legs. Then a stubby, red tail. A rather large calf lay in the straw with the umbilical cord wrapped around its neck.

"Allister, remove that cord!"

The cow lay panting for a moment or two. When Allister released the calf's head from the cord's loop, the baby gave a weak cry. Father let go of Bessie's head. The anxious mother got up to check on and lick her baby.

"They're out of danger now. You boys can go back to sleep. Got school this morning."

As they got back into bed, Allister exclaimed, "Wow! Wasn't that thrilling? To help a new life come after such a struggle?"

"I know. And the one who rescued Bessie's baby was me. Imagine that. I can hardly believe it myself."

"Who'd ever guess that you'd make such a great veterinarian, Jim!"

"Vet – a – what?"

"Veterinarian."

"What's that?"

"A special doctor for animals."

"Oh … guess I did tonight, didn't I?"

Allister was so excited about what he had seen and experienced that it took him quite a while to fall asleep.

———

When Mother woke Allister and Jim later that morning, Allister was so groggy he could hardly open his eyes.

"Come on, Allister, Jim. I let you sleep in a little, but you've got to get up now." She continued to stand next to their bed, apparently waiting until Allister put his feet on the floor. When he had, she said, "Allister, you boys did such a good job rescuing Bessie and her calf that Father says he will do your morning chores. You two can take a bath, wash your hair, and put on clean clothes before breakfast. Got everything ready for you. Now hustle. You don't want to be late."

After breakfast, the twins stopped in the barn on their way to school—Jim to check on the calf he helped save, and Allister to discover a piece to a puzzle.

"Father, if Jim hadn't been able to turn the calf around inside its mother, the baby wasn't the only animal that would have died. The cow would have died, too, wouldn't she?"

"Yes, son."

"How did you know about turning the baby around?"

"Because that's what the doctor did during Jessie's delivery. She was a breech birth baby. If he hadn't been successful, Mother and Jessie would have both died."

Allister gulped. "Oh."

"Better run along. I think I hear the school bell."

With his heart in his throat, and his mind in turmoil, Allister raced across the pasture and vaulted the fence. Once he was in the schoolyard, he slowed down. The story his father had just told Allister gave him a lot to think about! All this time, he had assumed that Jessie's handicaps were the result of no doctor at her delivery or a midwife with insufficient training who had made some big mistakes. If their Guernsey cow had never had her breech birth calf with Father in attendance, Allister would never have learned what had happened to Jessie. He had never heard his parents even mention how traumatic the birth of the youngest member of their family had been. Allister guessed that was because the negative possibilities of the difficult delivery had badly shaken them. The fact that Jim and he could have been without a mother horrified him. Not exactly sure about what to do with the thought, Allister tucked it way down inside himself. He had a full day of school to deal with just now.

After dinner that day, Allister lost more than an hour of history study at school. When he had stifled his tenth yawn and his eyelids had closed of their own accord, resting his head on his desk for a few minutes seemed the best idea. Waking up with a start later, he looked around the room at empty desks. Everyone including Jim had already gone home. "Sorry, Mr. Webster. I guess I fell asleep."

"That's alright, Allister. From Jim's story, I hear you two had an amazing experience last night … one you'll remember the rest of your lives."

"Yes, sir. In more ways than one. See you tomorrow."

"Goodbye, Allister." Mr. Webster smiled.

Grabbing his history book and scribbler from his desk, and his coat from its hook under the clock, Allister gasped at the hour. Three thirty! He was late for calf watch.

Only after all the calves had safely arrived did Dan and John return home with the team of Clydesdales and Mr. McRuer's newer wagon empty. Good-natured story swapping took over the conversation at several meals. John joined Allister in calling his twin "Dr. Jim, the vet." Allister was equally amazed at John's willingness to help Will with a pioneer homestead starting "from scratch" all over again.

"Will discovered that it was a lot harder than he thought it would be," John said. "I'm sure that he has a better appreciation now for all of Father's hard work."

The Friday before Palm Sunday, Father came to school to talk to Mr. Webster as the students left the building. *What now?* Allister wondered as he climbed over the pasture fence and ran with Jim to the barn and chores.

Allister didn't have long to wonder why his father talked to the teacher. At supper that night, Father told them about his plan. "Jim and Allister, you're coming with John and me to Will's place for ten days. Cleared it with your teacher. Dan will stay to help Mother with things here."

Allister remembered Will's farewell over a month ago. *So this is what he meant when he said "See you in April."*

"When do we leave?" Jim asked.

"Tomorrow morning."

Looking at his delighted twin, Allister could only groan inside himself. *Jim won't mind missing school, but I will*, he thought. *Good that it'll only be four days. The rest is Easter vacation.* "But we'll miss Good Friday and Easter Sunday services," Allister objected.

"Sorry, son. Helping your brother get a decent start on his claim is very important."

The next morning, Mother stuffed several wooden packing crates with a dinner for their trip and food for the week. Father hitched the team to the wagon that had already been loaded with additional lumber and cordwood. While Mother and John loaded the crates, blankets, Father's tools, and feed for the horses, Father helped Dan refit Mother's buggy with its wheels and canopy. "Guess you're all set," Father said, giving Mother a hug and a peck on her cheek. "Dan, take care of your mother and sister. See you in about a week."

John picked up Jessie, gave her a squeeze, and put her in Dan's arms.

The mud on the roads and the snow and ice melt in the river made the trip with a wagon load of lumber take a little longer than Father had counted on. Since they were still in Cherry Creek picking up supplies around dinner time, Father changed his mind about a picnic and treated his sons to a hot meal at the local hotel. As they rumbled north of town along a well-worn trail, Allister wondered what he'd see when they got there. *Does Will even have a house? Or is he still sleeping in a tent made from a tarpaulin? Father bought a hand pump at the Cherry Creek hardware store. Does that mean Will doesn't even have a well yet? What's he doing for water?*

chapter twelve

Shanty Shelter

In late afternoon, the McRuers' team of Clydesdales, Jake and Maggie, pulled their wagon next to a wood-frame shanty that had a shingle roof and walls with holes where windows and doors should be. John's hello was greeted with silence. A horse whinnied and Maggie answered.

From his wagon seat, Allister could see an open shed with a paddock in front, a miniature hill of gravel next to a stack of lumber, and Will's walking plow stuck in a furrow in a partially turned field. Will's wagon and the shorthorns were missing.

"Guess Will's out," John said. "Let's unload the lumber and hobble the horses so they can graze. Hobble the colt, too. He'll be happy to go with his mother."

While Father and John unloaded wood, Allister and Jim carried crates of food and the blankets to Will's shanty. When the twins elbowed their way through the tarpaulin-covered entry, they were surprised to see four doorways. Front and back doors were to be expected, as was one into the bedroom. But what was the fourth in the north wall for?

Peeking into the second room, Allister saw that Will's iron bedstead was its only piece of furniture. "Good thing John and Dan helped Will build furniture. Otherwise, this place would have nothing in it."

Allister and Jim deposited their blankets and extra clothes onto the floor in a corner of the main room. Thinking, *Glad I'm not Will. Wouldn't like to live in such sparse circumstances*, Allister opened the one cupboard that stood against the north wall and put away the food supplies Mother had sent with them.

Although the shanty wasn't exactly clean, Will's place didn't look as messy as another bachelor's place Allister had seen.

"Jim, if you'll split some kindling and build a fire, I'll get some water." Grabbing an empty bucket that rested on the table, Allister went outside to ask where he might get some. As far as he could see, Will's homestead had no well yet. There was no longer any snow that could be melted, either.

"A creek is about a quarter mile that way," John said, pointing. "But don't fill just one bucket." He placed a wooden yoke across Allister's shoulders and hooked a bucket to the ropes that hung from each end. "A neighbour showed Will how to use this shoulder yoke," John said, answering Allister's question before he could ask.

When Allister returned with the water, he poured it into the large wooden tub that sat in the corner of the paddock. The shorthorns would be thirsty when they got back. After several trips, he took two full buckets into the shanty, poured one of them into a pot, and set it on the stove. *Boiling water will be ready for tea in time for supper*, Allister thought with satisfaction. His main task complete, he dropped into a chair to rest for a moment. *Whew! Even if the yoke puts the weight of the buckets on my shoulders instead of my arms, carrying so many of them that far is tiring. If Will were to ask me for project suggestions, I'd say dig a well. Not that he'd ever ask me for my opinion.*

Going outside to see what else John or Father might want him to do, Allister overheard John say, "Father, you're used to being in charge, but remember whose place this is. Our week together will go much more smoothly if you're willing to do things Will's way—even when you think he's wrong."

Allister couldn't believe his ears. Is John daring to advise Father?
"And ..."

"What, Angus?" Father growled, glaring at his oldest son.

"Don't give Will any advice unless he asks for it."

Father harrumphed and spat out, "I'll thank you to keep your opinions to yourself."

Unfolding his arms, Father picked up some cordwood. When he turned around and saw Allister standing there, Father handed him the wood. "Come on, son. Help us stack this near the back door. Anybody seen Jim?"

"He's over by the horses," John said.

Carrying the armful of wood to the shanty, Allister mulled over John's suggestions. *Hope Father gives in and actually follows the advice; otherwise, sparks will fly. Will is the most head-strong of all us boys.*

After stacking all the wood and filling the bin next to the stove with kindling, Father, John, and Allister sat in Will's shanty, drinking tea and monitoring the reheating of Mother's savoury-smelling beef stew from a couple of her canning jars. As the sun sank below the western line of prairie grass, the plod of cattle hooves and the squish of wheels in mud brought everyone outside. Will was back.

"Hello, everyone. So glad you're here!" Will said, grinning. "See you've made yourselves right at home."

"Uh huh. You're just in time for supper." John stepped over to remove the yoke from the shorthorns.

"Where's the colt?"

"Out grazing with his mother and Jake," Father said.

Will put his team in the paddock and walked back to the shanty.

"Allister, go tell Jim it's supper," Father said.

During the meal, Mr. McRuer and John occupied the only chairs. Everyone else sat on an upside-down packing crate.

"Went to Elgin," Will said between slurps. "Got hinges, pieces of glass, cans of beans, and some soap and oatmeal. Tried to bargain for a second-hand harrow. Didn't have enough cash. Fellow wanted too much. Father, I have some good news. One of my neighbours has hired me to help with his herd of milk cows. That's income until I get a crop sold."

As Will took another sip from his cup of tea, a look of frustration flickered across his face. "But taking that job has slowed the work on my own place. Now that you all are here, I can really use your help. Glad for all the things that Mother sent from her cellar, too."

"Thought so!" John teased. "You haven't missed us at all! Just Mother's cooking!"

"Well," Will admitted, his face turning a little pink. "Guess that's somewhat true. Haven't enjoyed doing my own laundry, either."

"Guess Mother's spoiled us all," Father agreed with a chuckle. "Before the rest of you came west, Angus and I used to argue over who'd do our washing."

"Well, there's only one person to do it here ... me."

"Will, what do you want us to tackle tomorrow?" John asked, changing the subject.

"The well. Getting tired of hauling water."

I couldn't agree more, Allister thought, rubbing his shoulders.

"Good thing I only have three animals to haul it for," Will continued. "That reminds me. Jim, better turn out the shorthorns to graze."

The next morning, Allister got up to stretch. *I hope Father slept better on Will's bed. This wooden floor makes a most uncomfortable place to sleep.*

Will had evidently left to do his milking job before anyone else was up. By the time he returned with a pail of milk, Allister had helped John and Jim make a breakfast of oatmeal, scrambled eggs, slices of Mother's bread with butter, and hot tea.

After breakfast, Jim went to check on the animals. Father, John, and Will collected tools. Standing in the middle of Will's claim, Father surveyed the lay of the land. Allister groaned inside himself when he saw his father walk over to a spot and stick his shovel in the dirt. "Will, you'll probably want to put your well and later your windmill right here."

"No, actually, Father, I want it here." Will stood four feet from the north side of his shanty, opposite the "extra" doorway.

Allister held his breath, fully anticipating a row between Father and Will.

"Really, son? Right next to your house? That makes no sense at all."

"Look," Will shouted and strode towards Father, his fists doubled. "Whose claim are we working on? Yours, or mine?"

John moved to stand between his parent and his sibling. Allister approached his father and tugged at his sleeve. "Remember what John suggested earlier?"

Father frowned and harrumphed. Minutes ticked by. Will continued to glare at his father and stand with his fists clenched.

Finally, Father's shoulders relaxed. He walked over to the spot Will had indicated. "Alright, son. We'll put it where you want it."

John motioned to Allister. "Until we need your help, better haul more water."

Shouldering the wooden yoke with its dangling buckets, Allister trudged to the creek. Relief swept over him. *Whew! Good thing Father backed down and followed John's advice. I'm so glad this confrontation ended peacefully. Hope there won't be another one.*

On a second trip to the creek, Allister was surprised to see a herd of black and white cows. Leaning on a pole nearby was their bushy-bearded herdsman. Sitting next to him was a pint-sized, long-haired, black and white dog. "Hello, young fellow. You my new neighbour?"

"No, sir," Allister answered. "Your new neighbour is Will, my older brother. Our father, two of my other brothers, and I have come to help Will with his new place."

"Wonderful. Starting out's always a bit of a job. Name's Randy. What's yours?"

"Allister."

"Nice to meet you, Allister. Have a suggestion for you, if I may? Draw your water a little upstream from here. This is where my brother and I frequently water our herds. Upstream the water will be fresher and cleaner."

Seeing the cows stir up mud from the bottom of the creek, Allister nodded and hefted his buckets upstream. As he hauled his full buckets back up the bank, he heard the herdsman whistle. Turning around, Allister watched as man and dog ranged behind the herd, driving them towards a fenced pasture.

The rest of the day, everyone worked on the well. As the shaft got deeper, Jim and Allister took turns in its depths, filling buckets with dirt that Father hauled up. Will and John cut three-foot-long boards and nailed them onto four long posts that they lowered into the hole as a liner ... to prevent cave-ins, Will said. As the diggers removed dirt below, gravity pulled the square, wooden liner down, and Will or John added boards to its top.

From the bottom of the shaft, Allister glanced from time to time at the four walls of liner surrounding him. While bits of dirt trickled between the boards now and again, he realized with relief that he was in less danger now than he had been last summer. *I'm safer digging Will's well than I was when I helped dig the well in front of the school. The soil there was sandier, and a cave-in had been possible at any time. Will's shaft liner seems to be working well.* Allister quickly filled the bucket beside him. *Guess I don't need to worry.*

After a hot bean, bread, and tea dinner break, the well digging resumed. The afternoon trotted by. Buckets of dirt piled up, and their hole got deeper and deeper. An hour before sunset, Will excused himself to go to his milking job.

When Will left, Mr. McRuer sent Allister and Jim to fetch the livestock. With ropes looped over their shoulders, the twins trotted in the direction that Jim had come back from that morning. Hoof prints and cropped stems showed where their animals had been, but they weren't there.

"Where do you suppose they went?" Allister mused.

For half a mile, the twins followed a trail of bent grass and muddy hoof prints. A cluster of animals stood in the distance. Jim whistled and called Jake and Maggie by name. The mare turned and whinnied but didn't come.

"Something's wrong," he said.

Both Clydesdales were pacing back and forth along the top of the creek bank. The shorthorns stood nearby.

"Look," Allister said, peering over the edge, "the colt seems to be stuck at the bottom. Hope he hasn't broken a leg."

Allister and Jim slid down the bank and sloshed into the creek. The yearling was scared and sweaty from his unsuccessful efforts to climb up. At first, he wouldn't let either boy touch him. Jim talked to the colt, and Maggie stood at the top of the bank, nickering. After several minutes, Jim was able to put a rope halter over the young horse's neck and nose. "Here, Allister, hold this. Stroke his neck. When he calms down, I should be able to examine him."

Allister held the halter while Jim ran his hands up and down the animal's legs.

"He appears sound," Jim said. "But I need to remove his hobbles. They and the slippery bank are the reasons he can't get out."

In moments, the colt's front legs were free. As Allister led the colt upstream, Maggie walked along the top of the bank ahead of them. At one point, she stopped. Allister took the hint and led the colt up the slope. The three of them headed back across the prairie. Allister took out his handkerchief and wiped his brow. *Whew! That was close. I was so afraid this young one would panic and break his leg. A horse with a broken leg would have to be put down. That would have been a huge loss for Will. I know he's counting on the colt to become his main draft horse when the shorthorns get too old to break sod.*

Shortly after Allister had put the colt in Will's paddock, Jim returned, leading Jake with the shorthorns following. Pouring some mounds of feed on the ground inside the fence, the twins lured the cattle into the paddock and closed the gate. With the livestock secure, Jim ran to tell Father about the colt's rescue. Mr. McRuer came to have a look. He ran his hands over the yearling's legs. "Good thing you found them and managed to get him out. He seems fine."

A sense of relief swept over Allister. "How's the well coming?" he asked.

"Down many feet," Father said. "No water yet, but we'd better quit now. Out of daylight, temperature's dropping, and wind's picking up. Those low clouds along the northwestern horizon could mean snow."

"Oh, boy!" Allister said. "With no windows or doors in place, Will's shanty won't be much of a shelter against a storm."

"You're right, Allister. Boys, get some boards and tools. We've got doors to build."

While tea water and oatmeal heated on the stove in Will's shanty, Allister took the opportunity to shed his wet socks and boots and change into dry pants. *Ah! That feels better. My feet were freezing.* He looked at Jim. "Well, Mr. Soggy, aren't you going to get out of your wet things?"

"Leave me alone, Allister. You're not Mother." In spite of his protest, Jim sat down to remove his boots.

John and Father set up boards on sawhorses. With their only light coming from one kerosene lamp and a barn lantern, they worked on a front door. "Will talked about getting hinges. Angus, do you know where he put them?"

Before anyone could move, a hand holding some hinges came out of the dark. "Had them in my coat pocket."

"Oh, hi, Will. Didn't hear you come," John said.

"With all the sawing and hammering, I'm not surprised."

"We've taken it upon ourselves to make you a few doors," Father said.

"Storm's brewing. Should hit before morning," John added.

"I know."

"Jim and I brought in the animals," Allister said. "They have feed and water."

"Good."

Jim stuck a finger in the oatmeal and yanked it out. "Ow! Supper's hot! Let's eat."

After supper, Will left the shanty and returned in a few minutes with two window frames and a bucket with pieces of glass in it.

"How do you want the frames put in?" Father asked.

"Hinged to the top of the window jamb. That way I can swing them up to open or drop them down to close."

"I'll get the jamb ready for the hinges if you and the twins will put glass in the frames," Father offered. He searched among his tools until he found a hammer and a chisel.

Several hours later, the five McRuers put in place a front door and a window in the front wall of the shanty, stopping the wind and snow from whistling through those openings. As soon as the west window in the bedroom was also hinged and locked in, Will excused himself to go to bed. Storm or not, he had his milking job to do at dawn.

Father and three sons continued building. Before they were finished, however, Jim and Allister were nodding and yawning. "Sorry, Father. We can't keep our eyes open."

"That's alright, Allister," Father said. "You boys go to bed."

Before he crawled under his blanket to sleep on the floor, Allister put on a dry pair of socks and propped his soggy boots and socks near the stove. Jim copied.

When Allister woke the next morning, the wind over the prairie was still a howling, icy monster. But Will's shanty was pleasantly warm. A door closed the extra hole in the north wall, and the back door had been built and installed in the east wall. Will's only cupboard had been moved to block off the open window jamb next to the back door.

From the snoring coming from the bedroom, Father must still be sleeping, Allister thought. He got up, stretched, and tiptoed to see where John was. Father and son were sleeping back to back in Will's bed. John must have crawled in after Will got up. The bedroom's door leaned against the east wall, temporarily closing off the remaining window opening.

Moving quietly to the stove, Allister stoked its embers into flame and filled the firebox. The water buckets were empty. Opening the back door, he faced a scene of whirling white. A foot of heavy, wet snow already covered the ground, and the storm was showing no signs of letting up. *I guess we drink snow melt today*, he thought as he filled a bucket from the bank behind the shanty. *Hope Will doesn't get lost in this stuff. None of us would have any idea where to look for him.*

When Allister re-entered the room, Jim began to stir. "Good morning, sleepy head," Allister teased. "I'm actually up before you. Can you believe that?"

"Must be some sort of miracle!" Jim mumbled. "Hey, it's warm in here!" He sat up and looked around. "Thought we'd all be frozen to death by morning!"

"Come to think of it, Will would've been if we hadn't been here to help."

"That's for sure," John's voice came from the bedroom. "Aren't you glad you came, Allister?"

Before Allister could respond, Father's voice boomed from the bed. "Jim, Allister, go check on the animals. Put more feed and what's left of the hay down for them."

For the rest of the day, Allister worked with his father and brothers to make and install the remaining windows and hang the bedroom door.

Late afternoon, the storm quit. Before Will left that evening for his milking job, he went outside to stake the outline of the shed he wanted built over the well and its hand pump.

First, he insisted on the well close to his house, Allister thought. *Now he wants a shed built over it? Will sure has some strange ideas.*

chapter thirteen

From Scratch

While Will explained what he wanted, Allister held his breath. *I don't understand why. Father probably doesn't either. Hope Father doesn't argue about it, though. We already know once Will has made up his mind, he won't change it just because Father says he should.*

But Father didn't comment while Will talked, and Allister felt his tension ease from his chest, trickle down his legs, and ooze out his toes.

After Will left to go to his milking job, John fetched a couple of shovels so the snow could be cleared from the area around the well. Father asked Allister and Jim to find four large rocks and bring a long rope and a dozen boards.

"Allister, tie the rope around this rock," Father said. "Let's see if our well has any water yet."

After allowing the rock to touch the bottom of the shaft, Father pulled it up. Both the rock and six inches of rope were wet. "Almost deep enough. Finish it tomorrow. Let's get started on the pump house."

Following instructions, Allister, Jim, and John set the rocks into the ground to support the four corners of the shed walls. By nightfall, they had built a frame of studs for the shed and nailed it to the outside of the north wall of the shanty.

"I wonder if Will means to haul water across his main room floor out to his animals," Father said.

———◆———

The next morning after Will had returned from milking and they had eaten breakfast, Father sent Jim to herd the animals to graze what grass they could by pawing through the rapidly melting snow. Allister hauled buckets of the cleanest snow he could find to melt for drinking water.

By noon, Will, shoeless and with pants rolled up, had cleared an additional foot of mud from the bottom of the well. John had cut and nailed more boards to the top of the well liner. "Let's keep the liner about a foot above the water level in the well," Will said. "John, better attach some horizontal braces to the boards at the top so it can't drop any further. I don't want my water to taste like rotting wood."

At dinner that noon, everyone sat close to the stove with their boots off, trying to warm up and dry off. Allister couldn't stop shivering. *Don't know if I'll ever get warm. And to think that I'll have to put my cold, wet boots back on, later.* He shuddered.

Sloshing around in wet snow or cold mud for hours had chilled everyone's body and heated a few tempers, especially Will's. "Aaalliiisss, you should've been the one in the bottom of the well this morning," Will started in.

Allister rolled his eyes. *What? I am just as miserable as Will is. Yet I'm here—helping him. And he thinks he has the right to find fault with me?* Wrapping his arms around his legs, Allister bit his tongue to keep from adding hot oil to Will's fiery words.

"No, not him!" John broke into what could have been another of Will's tirades. "Don't want him getting a fever from the cold."

"But it's alright for me," Will complained bitterly.

"Do you imagine for a minute," Jim chimed in, "that I enjoy sloshing around in the cold and wet any more than you, Will?"

"Son, Angus and Jim are right." Father glared at Will. "Remember, it's your well! You are the one who chose to start this claim at this time of year."

"Besides, you're a man ... taller, definitely stronger," John said, seeming to reason with Will once again. "Allister's yet a boy. Why do you always expect him to do as much as you can? Be fair! Just so you know, brother of mine, we're all cold and miserable right now ... me, too!"

Allister smiled at John. *Big brother to the rescue again. Whatever would I do without him? Father defended me, too. Didn't expect him to. Never know if or when he will.*

Silence fell on the group as they sipped cups of tea and did their best to absorb the warmth of the stove. An hour later, warmed but not exactly dry, they returned to the work on the well. Testing its water depth one more time, Father said he thought it was deep enough. At Will's direction, they hauled and dumped the entire hill of gravel into the well. "That'll help settle the mud at the bottom," Will said. "Learned that from a neighbour."

They built a wide platform over the top of the well and set the hand pump with its pipe in place. While they built the shed over the pump, Father asked, "Will, you sure you want to haul water through your house to the animals? That seems terribly impractical to me."

"Haul water through my house?" The volume of Will's voice rose with each word. "Whatever gave you that idea?" He was practically shouting by the time he finished his question.

"Three walls around the well, attached to the house." Father lowered the hammer in his hand. "One door ... into the house, Will."

"Oh," Will muttered. "Guess I forgot to tell you that I wanted another door built into the east wall of this shed. That way the coldest, northwesterly prairie winds won't be able to blow directly into my shed."

"Good solution, son."

"The purpose of the shed and its door into the shanty," Will explained, "is to prevent pump freeze up. When it's too cold outside, I can open the door that's in the north wall of the house to let heat from the stove into the pump's shed. Hopefully the heat from the house will warm the pump enough to stop it from freezing, even in the bitterest weather of January, and I'll never have to melt snow for water."

Father's eyebrows went up in total surprise.

Ah ha! Allister thought. *Will remembers what we had to do a couple of months ago when our well froze up. Chopping kindling and melting enough snow for drinking water for all our animals as well as us was backbreaking work. Will's idea isn't strange. It's brilliant!*

When the pump shed was completed, Allister, Jim, and John worked together on digging post holes for pasture fencing. Father helped Will build a frame for a four-stall barn.

Around the supper table that evening, Will worried aloud about his dwindling pile of lumber. "My job is morning and evening every day of the week. Can't very well take off for a month to cut my own lumber on Turtle Mountain."

"Does Elgin have a lumber yard?" Father asked.

"No. Cherry Creek has the closest one, but …"

"Then when you get back from work tomorrow morning, we need to take both wagons to town for more lumber."

"But …"

"Don't have the money for two loads of lumber?" John asked.

"Well … not even one." Will stood and with a grimace and pulled his empty pants' pockets out.

Jim chortled.

Allister ducked his head to hide a wide grin. *A clown? A complainer? What is Will this time?*

"You think I'm being funny?" Will growled with a glare at Jim.

"Don't worry about the money, son. Angus and I both brought some with us. We'll pay for it."

"Umm. Alright, but it's a loan. Pay you back as soon as I can."

Late the next afternoon, Will drove Father's team of Clydesdales and a wagon full of lumber into the middle of the farmyard. Dropping their shovels, Jim and Allister ran over. "Where's Father?"

"He's an hour or so behind me. Cattle are slower than horses, so he sent me ahead. I had to get back in time to do the milking."

Peering into the wagon bed, Allister saw fence posts and poles. "This load's for your pasture fence, eh?"

Will nodded and handed the reins over to Jim.

"We'll take it from here, Will," Jim said. "See you at supper."

Jim and Allister climbed aboard and drove the load out to the fence line. John trotted over and helped them deposit the poles and posts along the row of holes that they'd already dug. When the wagon was empty, the twins rode it back to the paddock. After removing harnesses and grooming the horses, the twins turned Jake and Maggie in with the colt.

Just before dark, Father and shorthorns plodded up the farm lane, stopping in front of the barn frame. Removing their yoke, he put the cattle in with the horses and scooped out feed for all five animals.

When Will returned from milking, a supper with hot tea was ready. Since the snow storm, everyone came in every day hungry, grumpy, muddy, and wet at least to their knees. The now- slushy snow made puddles and oozing mud unavoidable.

Allister had to admit to himself that he was more miserable than he ever remembered being. *Will I or my boots ever get completely dry? Don't think so. Will I ever do what Will is doing? Start my own homestead from scratch? If it goes anything like this one has … never.* Draping his soggy pants over a chair and setting them and his boots close to the stove that evening to dry overnight, he was glad he had brought a change of clothes. Sleeping back to back with Jim under two blankets, he was dry and warm by morning, much to his surprise.

When he woke up at dawn, Allister had to stifle a laugh to avoid disturbing the others. Will's main room looked like a laundry with pants hanging everywhere. His father and brothers had copied him.

For two days, Allister worked with Jim and John on the pasture fence. Gradually, the barn frame filled in with window and door jambs and rafters to start its roof. Midafternoon on Friday, Allister saw a buggy pull up next to the paddock. The driver got out and tied his horse to the railing, and then stepped around to the other side to help a woman out.

Allister dropped the fence pole he was carrying. "John, Jim, we've got visitors."

John hustled to tuck in his shirt and hitch up his pants. "Looks like we're taking a break, boys."

Allister hung back to let Will play host. But when the driver turned around, Allister flashed him a smile. It was Randy, the neighbouring herdsman.

"Hello, I'm Will."

"I'm your neighbour, Randy. This is my wife, Rachel."

While Will introduced his family to the couple, Allister studied the woman. Rachel, like her husband, was in her mid-forties. With her auburn hair wrapped in a braided bun at the nape of her neck, she was dressed in a simple, long-sleeved, ankle-length, green gown. When she shook Allister's hand, the twinkle in her gray-blue eyes won him over completely.

After glancing around at Will's homestead-in-progress, Rachel reached into her buggy for a large pot and quickly stepped towards the front door of his shanty. "We've brought you some supper for later and pie to share with you now," she said.

"Thank you, but my place is a little …"

"Don't worry, Will. Randy and I lived in a sod house with a dirt floor for some years when we first came out here a decade ago. A little mud doesn't scare me a bit."

Will raced ahead of her. Allister envisioned his brother grabbing all the hanging pants and throwing them onto his iron bedstead. When Allister heard the slamming of the bedroom door, he was sure of it. Chuckling, he followed the others into the shanty.

Rachel entered the main room, set her pot on the stove, and took the pie from her husband to set it on the table. She sat down in the chair Will offered her as if she'd been invited into the sitting room of a palace. "Thank you, Will," she said, smiling broadly at him. Her husband sat in the only other chair.

Stoking the stove under a pot of water, Will made tea for his guests. Soon everyone had a cup of hot drink and a tin plate of custard pie. Father and sons sat on a couple of upside-down crates or on the floor.

Allister savoured every bite of Rachel's pie. *Better even than Mother's.*

"What's behind that door, if I may ask?" Randy asked, pointing.

Will got up and opened the door in the north wall not far from the stove.

Randy's jaw dropped in surprise at seeing a pump inside a shed attached to the shanty.

Father and Randy were in the middle of discussing the virtue and drawback of Will's water works when Rachel got Will's attention to ask, "Excuse me, but where's your privy?"

"Sorry, Rachel. I don't have one yet."

"No matter. I'll make do," she said. She quietly left and a short time later re-entered the shanty through the back door.

Towards the end of their visit, Randy cleared his throat and, looking at his wife, said, "Rachel and I'd like to invite you to our place for Easter Sunday service. Several families meet in our home every Sunday morning for worship. You'd be welcome to join us."

Will glanced at John and Father. Folding his arms across his chest, he said, "I'm sorry, but we're rather busy right now. Don't think we've got the time."

Will wouldn't say this if Mother were here, Allister thought. *Is Father really going to go along with Will and put work ahead of church? He might do that during harvest, but now?* Allister blurted, "Father, could I go?"

Father looked at Will who, with a disgusted look on his face, shrugged. He started to open his mouth, but with a sharp look from John, shut it.

"Alright, son, you can go," Father said. "Would you like to, too, Jim?"

"No, but thank you for the invitation," he explained to the couple. "Have projects to finish before we head home. Allister and I need to return to school soon."

"School?" Rachel said. "That's wonderful. Glad to hear you have one."

"Yes, we helped build it last summer. Opened last August." Allister smiled.

"Well, I'm sure your neighbours are delighted," she said. "Many children of pioneer homesteads haven't had any education, except what their parents could give them at home. That was true for our own family."

Rachel and Randy have children, Allister thought. *Wonder if any of them are my age? Get to meet them day after tomorrow. Good.*

"Better be going," Randy said, rising. "See you Sunday morning, Allister."

After their visitors left, everyone went back to their work. Supper that evening had the special homemade taste of Rachel's creamed chicken with peas and dumplings.

"Now that's cooking!" John said.

"We miss our womenfolk, don't we, boys?" Father commented.

———————

By Saturday evening, Father and Will had boarded and shingled half the barn roof. Allister, Jim, and John had completed Will's pasture fence. Its sturdy gate had been made, but not hung. Will had yet to get hinges strong enough to bear its weight.

After supper when everyone had already gone to bed, Allister stayed up to pour warm water from a pot on the stove into the wash basin and rub himself clean. Not much could be done for his boots, he decided. Even if he cleaned them now, they'd pick up plenty of mud going cross-country between the farms.

While Allister got ready for his visit to the neighbours' farm, he thought about Randy's invitation. *Never heard of holding church in a home before. Wonder who will be there? What will they do? How will Easter at Randy's be different from such a service at Wood Lake School? In any case, it'll be a welcome break. Just wish Jim was coming with me.*

chapter fourteen

Finding Home

When Allister approached the front of Randy's home, he was greeted by the bark of the tail-wagging, black and white dog. Standing on the porch of the two-storey, wood-frame farmhouse, he knocked and waited. There was no response from inside. He wasn't sure what he should do.

Walking around back, he heard voices coming from the barn. When he investigated, he found Randy and his family working with their milk cows.

"Hello, Allister. You're a little early. Be done here shortly," Randy said, then introduced him to his children.

As Allister greeted the three boys and a girl, he realized that all of the young people were older than he was, even the youngest boy. *Still, they seem nice enough. Too bad our homesteads are so far apart.*

"We all help with the milking on the Lord's Day," Rachel explained, "so it's finished in time for meeting."

Sometime later, when Allister and Randy's family walked in the back door of the farmhouse, other people were coming in the front.

"Allister, sit here next to me," Randy said as everyone took their places in the large sitting room. Several dozen chairs were arranged in a double row around a small table that stood in the middle of the room. On the table was a loaf of bread and a large cup. The girls and small children sat with the women on one side of the room. The men and boys sat on the other. All the women and girls wore scarves, and many of the men sported thick beards.

An older man got up and passed out song books.

"Allister, did you bring a Bible?" Randy whispered.

"No, I didn't," he whispered back. *Besides*, he thought, *our family Bible is too big to carry around*.

"Brother Peter," Randy murmured to the grey-bearded man when he came around with a song book, "our guest, Allister, needs a Bible."

With two books in his hands, a Psalter and a leather-bound Bible, Allister waited to see what would happen. *Evidently, Brother Pete isn't the pastor or preacher of this church-in-a-house. I wonder who is. No man in special robes to lead. Definitely not a Presbyterian service, like the one we McRuers go to in our school. This service already appears to be like no other I've ever attended.*

After a period of absolute silence, first one man and then another stood to suggest a song, giving its title and number in the book. One of the other men started each song and everyone joined in, except Allister. Although Randy helped him find the pages, Allister could only read silently and listen. He'd never heard any of the tunes before.

> "Bearing shame and scoffing rude,
> in my place condemned He stood,
> Sealed my pardon with His blood;
>   Hallelujah, what a Saviour!"

Long after the group in Randy's sitting room had sung it, Allister read and reread this verse. Its words about Jesus' sacrifice for him in particular made Allister feel as if he needed these very words to find their home in his heart. *Is understanding their meaning a key to "making room in my heart for Jesus," like Reverend Fisker at the Burnside church suggested one Christmas?*

After the singing, several men stood up one at a time to read a section from a chapter of the Bible. Each time, Randy helped Allister find the passage in the book so he could read for himself and not just listen. At one point, an older man stood and talked about the meaning of a sentence in the Bible and how he had applied it to his life.

Allister remained puzzled as he listened. *So, no pastor. Yet all these men seem to know their Bible well. How? Study on their own?*

After almost an hour, a man near the table got up and broke in half the loaf of bread that was on it. He gave one part to the women, and the other to the men. As each person received it, he or she broke off a piece, ate it, and passed the loaf on.

"Allister," Randy whispered, "if you haven't received Jesus in your heart, I ask you to abstain."

At first, Allister was a little offended by this instruction. But then he noticed that not everyone was eating the bread. Most of the women and some of the men passed the pieces of loaf right over the heads of some of their children. The same was true when the cup was passed around. Everyone who ate a piece of bread also sipped from the one cup. Those who hadn't eaten, didn't drink.

After the meeting closed with a prayer and one last song, families left quietly, waiting until they had walked around behind the house to begin their visiting.

Allister followed Randy to the porch. "Allister, I'd like to explain our Lord's Table, our way of doing communion. When Jesus had His last supper with His twelve disciples, He passed around bread and wine and told His followers to remember His death that same way when He was no longer with them. Believers are instructed in the Bible to do this until He comes back. So that is what we do every Lord's Day."

"Randy, there's something else I don't understand. You don't seem to have a pastor or preacher."

"You're right. We don't. Every man is responsible to know his Bible and study it on his own, so he can lead his family and contribute to our meeting on the Lord's Day."

"I know about Anglican, Baptist, Presbyterian, and Catholic churches," Allister said. "Does your kind of church have a name?"

"We call ourselves Plymouth Brethren. There are several meeting places in Manitoba and Ontario that I know about." Randy smiled. "Might be more elsewhere."

"Do Plymouth Brethren always meet in a house?"

"Most of the time. Our groups are usually too small to afford a church building. And we don't have a school nearby where we could meet—like your family does."

About then, Allister realized he still had two books. Holding them out to give them back, he said, "I appreciate the loan, Randy."

"You keep the Bible. It's my gift to you," Randy said with a smile. "I would like our songbook back, though. We'd have a harder time replacing it."

"Thank you," Allister said, stuffing the Bible inside his shirt and wishing he had something to wrap it in. "Better get back. Not sure yet whether we leave for home this afternoon or tomorrow."

"Where's home?"

"A homestead that is east of Desford and north of Turtle Mountain."

"Goodbye. See you sometime. The Lord God knows when."

———

Sunday afternoon passed with no mention of the trip home. Allister's consternation grew as he listened to Will direct his father and brothers in how and where things were to be built.

When Will excused himself to do his milking job that evening, Allister quizzed John. "While I was at Randy's house this morning, did Father mention anything about when we'll be leaving?"

"No. Sorry, Allister. Not a word," John said.

Monday dragged along. Building on Will's homestead claim proceeded without pause. Still Allister heard nothing about going home. He pulled Jim aside. "Has Father said anything to you about heading back? Our Easter vacation is over."

"It is?" Jim shrugged. "Well, Father hasn't said anything about it to me."

Allister grew more anxious with each passing hour. At supper, Allister couldn't wait any longer. "Father, you promised Mother and Mr.

Webster that you'd have us back in time for school—today. Tomorrow is already Tuesday!"

"Allister, I'm sorry to have broken my word. In a day or two we'll be done with the major building projects, right Will?"

"Let me see," Will said, seeming to take a perverse delight in Allister's consternation. "Well—dug, pump—working, pump house—up, windows and doors to my house—complete, pasture fence and gate—not quite, barn—almost."

"What's left?" Allister demanded, feeling ready to explode.

"Hang pasture gate, construct outhouse, build and install windows and doors of the barn, finish the barn loft, plow ..."

"Whoa, son," Father interrupted. "I agree that between your job and those acres of unbroken prairie grass on your claim, you have your work cut out for you. I'm aware that spring planting is right around the corner. We'll help you complete the outhouse, pasture fencing, and the barn, but after that you're on your own."

Allister couldn't believe his ears! *We've already done so much. But Will wants more? And Father is going along with some of it?*

Reaching the end of his patience, Allister jumped to his feet and ran from the shanty, slamming its door behind him. Walking down the farm lane, he fumed. *Why is it that the only work the men in my family show any respect for is the physical kind? What about all the time and brains it takes to be successful in school? And why isn't Jim even more upset than I am? He's even less able to miss school than me!*

After a few minutes, Allister reached the end of Will's homestead lane. Turning onto the main trail towards Cherry Creek and staring into the dark, Allister briefly entertained the thought of continuing his walk all the way home. But he knew it would take him days to go the distance on foot. Besides, he was exhausted.

Cooled off from his walk in the evening air, Allister headed back towards the shanty. *God, Reverend Wood told me not to be afraid to ask You for help, so I ask You to help Father and my brothers to care as much about my education as I do!*

When Allister woke up the next morning, John, the Clydesdales, and Father's wagon were gone. An hour before dinner time, John returned with another load of lumber and a bunch of hinges and locks that he spread on the table. "I had the blacksmith in Cherry Creek make these heavy duty hinges and latch according to Will's drawings. Allister, go get Jim. Let's hang that pasture gate."

Within the hour, the gate was up and the cattle and horses happily explored the provision and boundaries of their newly-fenced domain. Allister and Jim climbed the fence and sat on the top rail to watch.

"One more project complete," Allister muttered. "Wonder how much longer it'll be before we can head home?"

"Why are you in such a hurry to leave?" Jim asked.

Allister looked at Jim with exasperation. "I know you would rather build than study, but the problem is that we've missed so much school this year. During harvest last fall, it was two weeks. This spring, we've missed even more. When we do get back to school, we'll have to scramble through our studies to make up for all the time we've lost by spending additional days doing Will's construction projects."

"Oh, right." Jim jumped down from the fence. "Forgot about that."

"Allister," Father said at their noon meal two days later, "almost finished with the barn. We can leave soon. You and Jim pack up our things while we take care of the last few items."

Left in the shanty by themselves, Allister and Jim looked around at the shambles. Excited at the prospect of going home, Allister grabbed his dirty clothes and jammed them into an empty crate. "Well, don't just stand there, Jim. You heard Father. Pack up his and John's things. I'll pack ours."

Jim picked up a crate and went into Will's bedroom. The last item to go into Allister's crate was the Bible Randy had given him. Between the folds of his blanket, Allister nestled the book. *Now I have two books of my own—the one Mother gave me for Christmas, and my very own Bible.*

After the crates were loaded and stacked near the door, Allister turned to look at the main room of Will's shanty. Dirty dishes lay about. The kindling bin sat empty. Clumps of dried mud caked the floor. "Jim, we shouldn't leave our mess for Will to clean up. Let's split kindling and work on the floor while we heat more water to wash the dishes."

Jim grinned. "Be back in a minute."

Allister plopped an empty pot under the hand pump in Will's pump house. *Now what is Jim up to?*

When Jim returned, he was carrying two shovels.

"What in the world are those for?" Allister asked.

"The mud."

Allister laughed. "Good idea. Let's scrape away. Will's broom probably wouldn't be able to do an adequate job, and we don't have time to scrub the floor—like Mother would."

When he felt Will's shanty looked livable again, Allister helped Jim load the crates of their belongings into Father's now-empty wagon and harness Jake and Maggie.

Their chores complete, Allister and Jim ambled across the farmyard to see if Father and John had finished the homestead's construction projects to Will's satisfaction. Allister arrived in time to watch the installation of the barn's final half-door. While waiting for Father and John to load their tools into the wagon and hitch up the horses, Jim and Allister climbed up the loft ladder to have a look at the inside of the new barn.

"What a lot of work!" Allister said.

"You can say that again! Will's had the help of five of us! Little wonder it took Father three years to get ours built, since he did a lot of it by himself."

While Will thanked and said goodbye to the others, Allister scrambled into the wagon seat. As they headed out, Will called out, "I'm so glad you're finally leaving! You've eaten everything! There's nothing left!" And he took out his handkerchief, wiped his eyes, and blew his nose.

John and Jim just cracked up. They laughed all the way down the lane. Allister didn't know what to make of Will's behaviour at first, because he knew for a fact that there was still some food in the shanty's cupboard. *Well, what do you know,* he finally surmised. *My crabby brother has finally found his funny bone!*

The colt, however, wasn't happy to see them leaving. He trotted along the fence, whinnying as he watched his mother and buddy Jake disappear once again.

Settling into the seat beside Father, Allister began to hum a tune that had been running in and out of his head at odd times since Sunday. *What is that song?* he thought. Part way to Cherry Creek, he recognized it as the song they had sung at Randy's house meeting in which each verse ended with "Hallelujah, what a Saviour!"

"Allister, you never did tell us much about the Easter service at Randy's house," Father said, hearing a snatch of the melody that slipped out of Allister's throat.

"Boy, was it ever different!" Allister began as he described Randy's house church.

———————

A little over an hour later, Jake and Maggie trotted into Cherry Creek. Returning with an almost empty wagon had speeded up the trip. Father drove the team to a spot beside the railroad tracks opposite of the train depot. Setting the brake, he climbed out of the wagon. "We need to rest the team for a bit. Let's go in the hotel restaurant for a drink."

When they were seated at a table, Father ordered lemonade for everyone. While they were sipping the cool drink, the manager came over. "Are you James McRuer?" When Father nodded, the manager said, "Mr. Mason's looking for you."

"Where is he?"

"Upstairs. Room 102."

"Thank you."

"You're welcome," the manager said as he left.

Father didn't budge.

"Aren't you going to see what he wants?" John asked, sounding annoyed.

"I think I know what he wants. Help building another school. And I don't want to volunteer any more time. I did plenty of that when we built Wood Lake School last summer."

"Maybe it's for pay this time. At least find out the situation."

While Father and John argued, Allister and Jim finished their drinks.

"Oh, alright," Father finally said. "Mason was a good supervisor and a decent man. Did a good job on our school. Guess I owe him at least that courtesy."

Father got up, went across the lobby, and climbed the stairs. Allister and his brothers followed right behind him. Father knocked on the door. When Mr. Mason opened it, he shook Father's hand, greeted John, Jim, and Allister warmly, and invited them in.

"Glad you got my message," Mr. Mason said. "We're looking for stone masons to build a new, six-room school for Cherry Creek. Town has already outgrown its two-room building. The local school board has authorized me to hire men to quarry or set the stone. Hear you have masonry experience. Could I interest you in such a job? It offers two dollars a day plus room and board for your stay in town while you do it."

Father stood with a frown on his face and his arms folded across his chest. "I've a farm to manage. It's almost planting season."

Allister held his breath, feeling panic rise up his chest. *If Father takes this job, I'll be planting instead of finishing a school year—again. Just like two years ago when we moved here. So that we could be in Manitoba in time for planting, Jim and I missed the last two months of school.*

"Well, give it some thought," Mr. Mason continued. "Could really use your expertise and your work ethic. We'd like to start building the first of May. Need quarry men as soon as possible, if you know anyone who could do that job."

"Alright. Let you know in a week."

"Fair enough. Thank you. Goodbye."

Father hustled them back to their wagon. As they climbed in, Father said, "Angus, sit with me. Need to talk."

Allister and Jim stretched out in the bed of the wagon. Allister tried to listen to Father and John's conversation. Gradually, both their voices and the rattle of the wagon faded. Next thing he knew, they were home.

Once there, Allister woke up just enough to hug Mother and Jessie and carry his Bible and blanket upstairs. He exchanged a clean nightshirt for his dirty duds and climbed into bed. He was *so* happy to be home! As he drifted off to sleep, he desperately hoped his father wouldn't take the job offer.

chapter fifteen

Spring Scramble

Having missed almost two weeks of school, Allister went to his desk the next morning a bit frantic. The first day back, Mr. Webster spent some extra time helping Allister get his head back into arithmetic, reading, penmanship, spelling, grammar, Manitoba history, and North American geography. Much to Allister's surprise, their forced break made Jim more willing to throw himself into completing Grade 7.

While Allister was getting ready to leave for school a few days later, he was surprised to see John's tent tarpaulin rolled up and lying on the kitchen table. A brand new toolbox with some of Father's stone cutting tools in it sat next to the back door.

"Where's John going?" Allister asked Mother.

"He's taking a job at the stone quarry near the Pembina River."

When John came back into the house to hug Mother goodbye, he put his hands on Allister's shoulders. Looking at his two brothers, John said, "Don't worry, boys. This job is only for a couple of months, and I'll come home every Saturday night."

But his brother's words in no way reassured Allister. *Mary's gone. Will's gone. John's gone. That means Jim and I'll have more chores to do. How will we ever finish our homework?*

After school that day, Allister went into the barn expecting to shovel manure out and pitch in clean straw, but it was already done. The water trough and buckets in the pens and stalls were full. In the house, someone had filled the kindling bin. Allister checked the tea kettle and the wash water pot on the stove. They were both full. *All of the chores are done. That's great! Since they are, I can get some of my homework done before supper.*

Halfway through his reading assignment, Allister heard a horse clop into the farmyard. Leaving his homework on the table, he went out to investigate who had come. It was Mother, returning in her buggy. Not seeing Jim nearby, Allister offered to help her with the horse. After unharnessing and grooming Shalazar, Allister turned him into their new back pasture. The gelding tossed his mane and raced around the pasture. Not finding his buddies, he stood at the fence nearest the plowed fields, whinnying. When Jake answered, Shalazar lay down in the grass and rolled, kicking his heels in the air.

Feeling an elbow pressed against his own, Allister turned to see Jim standing next to him at the fence rail. "I never tire of watching that horse," his brother said with a dreamy look in his eyes.

Allister grimaced. "After all of the trouble that animal has caused, I don't like or trust him."

At supper that evening, Allister approached his father to get more answers about what John was doing. "Father, does John know anything about quarrying stone?"

"Not much."

Allister looked at Mother and thought that the answer to his next question might worry her, but he had to ask anyway. "Isn't that going to make his job more dangerous?"

"Could. But the first few days you and Jim were back at school, I took Angus up on Turtle Mountain. I showed him how to quarry rock. Had him practice with my tools on some big boulders. That building supervisor, Mason, is smart. He'll buddy up a 'green horn' like Angus with a more experienced fella. Your brother will be fine!"

"What about you, Father? Are you going to take the masonry job in Cherry Creek?"

"Can't afford not to. Your mother, Dan, and I talked about it. Dan and I'll get the fields and garden ready. Then while John and I do mason work, Dan will be in charge of the planting. Allister, you and Jim can help him."

"What? Instead of school?" Allister felt his face flush with anger.

"No, Allister. Calm down." Father said. "I know how important school is to you, and I'm glad it is. I mean that; I want you to help Dan every day after school."

Allister gasped. *This father of mine is crazy. Does he believe we are super boys?* Allister sputtered, "Planting on top of chores? How will Jim and I ever have time to do our homework?"

Father winked at Mother. "Did you have any to do today?" he asked.

"No, they were already done. Who did them?"

Jessie puffed out her chest. "I did. Well … Mother, Dan, and I together."

"That's wonderful, Jessie," Allister said, thinking, *But how?* He was even more surprised than he let on.

Looking at Allister, Jim said, "Did an excellent job, too, didn't she?"

Jim gave Jessie a squeeze. "Well done, little sister. But I thought you were afraid of the big animals. You told me once you didn't want to work in the barn."

Jessie looked at Dan and Mother. "They take out the cows and horses, and then I do it. Hard work. When I'm tired, I sit down a little. But I do it."

Father must have asked her to help us out. Allister took a deep breath and let it out slowly. *My little sister is more capable than I thought she could be. Wonders will never cease.*

After supper, Allister returned to his book and scribbler that still lay open on the dining room table. Sitting on the opposite side, Jim settled into his arithmetic homework.

In a few moments, Jessie was at Jim's elbow. "Look," she said, pointing at a black slate with green lines painted on it. "Mother buy for me. Dan paint for me. Mother teach me my letters. I write my name."

Sticking her tongue out sideways as if she was concentrating really hard, Jessie carefully wrote her name in capital letters. Allister got up and walked around the table to stand behind Jessie. "Very good," he said. "How about numbers? Can you count?"

"One, two, three, five, four, nine, seven … ten," she said, slowly and deliberately, looking at Allister.

"Can you write them? Can you write one? Two?"

Jessie stuck out her tongue again as she struggled to write the numbers. The number two didn't look quite right. Three was backwards. She tried to write five, but couldn't. Jim took her dainty hand in his and helped her write the numbers four and five. "Jessie, you're doing so good. We're proud of you, aren't we, Allister?"

Allister smiled at his sister and nodded, but couldn't help thinking, *Apparently, Jessie can learn to do chores. But other types of learning are so hard for her. I wonder why? Mother was right to teach her at home. She knows how to go "Jessie speed."*

———◆———

The afternoon of the last day of April, Father had Dan drop him off at the main road to Cherry Creek. Since that road had frequent traffic, Father said he was sure he could catch a ride to town from there.

When Dan got back with Shalazar and the buggy, Allister asked, "Did Father say how long he's going to be gone?"

"Not sure. Until the school's built or harvest comes, whichever is first, I guess."

"But that's months from now!"

"I think we'll be fine. One hundred acres are plowed. I've gotten a good start on the harrowing. John promised to come home on the weekends. And Joe helps—worked with Mother and me on that south pasture fence while you were at Will's place."

———◆———

Each afternoon after school for the next four weeks, Allister and Jim changed clothes, gobbled a snack, and joined Dan in the fields. Each evening before supper, they drove the livestock from the south pasture to the barn for safe keeping. The calves would make easy prey for the wolves, coyotes, and lynx that still roamed nearby on Turtle Mountain.

In late May, Queen Victoria's birthday was celebrated with a three-day holiday weekend. But Allister didn't regard that Monday as a real vacation, because any "time off" from school meant work in the fields. With Father and John at home, everyone worked on Mother's garden or dragged logs from the mountain for firewood.

When May turned to June, the anticipation of examination-day seemed to make Mabel, Wood Lake School's only eighth grader, a bundle of nerves. Although she appeared calm, Allister was well aware of his schoolmate's anxiety. Mr. Webster finally took it upon himself to help her prepare. Allister, Jim, and Amy's school chores for two weeks involved keeping the first graders quietly busy and out of the teacher's hair. As he watched Mabel sweat her way through her exam preparation and did his best to keep his younger schoolmates occupied, Allister worried. *If I have to stop my studies to harvest, build, or plant for any length of time next school year, I'll never be able to pass my eighth grade exams. And if I can't pass them, I won't graduate.* The thought gave him a stomach ache.

At home that week and the next, there was the constant pressure of getting as much of their eighty acres of wheat planted as was possible after full days at school. This time, it was Allister who showed Jim how to work a mechanical seed broadcaster while Mother and Jessie played scarecrow and Dan followed with the harrow to cover the seed.

In the afternoons towards the end of the second week of planting, Allister could hardly keep his mind on his studies, or his eyes open. Working at farm and school from sun up to sun down was taking its toll. *I am so tired*, Allister thought. *Lying my head down on my desk to nap is tempting. Jim doesn't seem to be faring much better.* Out of the corner of his eye, Allister observed Jim's head snap up after slowly drifting downward.

That Friday evening, Allister was surprised and relieved when Father and John both showed up for supper. "Dan says you boys have been real troopers!" Father said.

"But we haven't finished sowing all the wheat. We haven't even started the oats," Jim sputtered. "And it's the third week in June already!"

"Don't worry. Father, Dan, and I will take it from here," John said. "We've asked for a few days off. You only have one more week of school, don't you?"

"Yes, but we don't go to school Monday. It's examination day for Mabel," Allister explained. "The district superintendent is coming to proctor her tests. We're to stay home and finish the projects that Jim and I have to hand in before the end of term."

"Well now," Father said, "looks like everyone has his assignment."

The next morning after helping Jessie with chores and eating breakfast, Allister laid out his homework on the dining room table. Jim soon joined him. "You would have to blab to Father about our unfinished projects, Allister!"

"Look, Jim, if I hadn't, we'd be expected to be out in the fields today, and we're almost out of time. On top of that, I'm almost completely out of steam. Don't know about you, but I'm plumb tuckered. One more day of field work from sun up to sun down, and nobody would be able to wake me up for a week!"

When Allister and Jim returned to school on Tuesday, Mabel was all smiles.

"You've passed your exams!" Allister guessed. "Congratulations!"

"Thanks to you and Jim! You two helped me a lot!"

"Passing the eighth grade means that you can go on to high school. Are you?"

"I'd like to, but when I asked my parents, they said no. The closest high school is in Brandon, seventy miles away. My parents say they don't want me to live far away from home in a big town with strangers, just so I can go to high school. So I guess this is the end of my schooling."

Feelings of dismay hit Allister hard while he listened to Mabel's description of her predicament. *Has she given up too easily? If I were in a similar situation, what would I do?* He then remembered that his father and older brother were working on Cherry Creek's new school. *Will it be done in time for school next fall? It's supposed to be bigger than the one the town already has. Will it include high school?*

———◆———

Thursday was Field Day at Wood Lake School. Several mothers brought a picnic meal and stayed to help organize the activities. There were the three-legged races, the burlap sack, and the egg-on-spoon contests.

Allister teamed up with Georgie for a three-legged race. It was the little boy's first time. Although Allister and Georgie had practiced before the race started, Georgie stumbled during the race and pulled Allister down with him. They had only gotten halfway across the schoolyard. Georgie burst into tears. "Sorry, Allister. Tried to make big steps like you."

"Don't worry about that." Allister sat up and put his arm around his young friend. "You did your best, Georgie. Maybe in another race, you'll win. But are you alright? You fell pretty hard. Did you hurt yourself?"

"Oh, ow. Allister, my knee hurts." With tears still spilling down his face, Georgie pulled up his pant leg.

"Hmm. Better go ask your mother to help you with your scraped knee. When you feel better, try another race."

Allister helped Georgie up. The little boy hobbled over to his mother, and Allister found another partner for the next race.

When it was time for the burlap sack challenges, the older students were divided from the younger ones. As Allister stood in his sack behind the line scratched in the dirt, he looked down the row of competitors: James, Teena, Mabel, Etta, Amy, and Jim. Mr. Webster yelled "On your mark! Get set! Go!"

Gripping the top edge of his sack, Allister leapt like a kangaroo towards the finish line scratched in the dirt along the opposite side of the schoolyard. At the beginning, Mabel was in front of everybody. Then Jim got ahead. Two-thirds of the way across, Allister saw Mabel and then Jim stumble and fall.

All of Wood Lake School chanted his name. "All-i-ster, All-i-ster!" With every hop Allister made, the yelling got louder. "ALL-I-STER!

ALL-I-STER!" Keeping his eyes on the goal, he jumped faster and faster. Just when his lungs felt ready to burst for lack of air, Allister jumped across the finish line and collapsed. A cheer went up and many hands thumped him on the back as he sat up.

"Congratulations, Allister! That was quite some race," Mr. Webster said, helping him to his feet. "By the end, you were the only one still standing!"

Allister grinned. *Praise from Mr. Webster doesn't come often. I can't believe I won. I even beat Jim.*

Moving along the edge of the schoolyard to get a better view of the next activity, Allister turned to look beyond the nearby pasture fence and across the fields of his father's homestead. *The school year is almost over. Most of my schoolmates are happy about that, especially Jim. Not me. Not looking forward to the endless farm work that will fill the long days of summer.*

The last race was the funniest one—the egg-on-spoon run for the six youngest children. Since the eggs were raw, some of them splattered yellow in the dirt or on bare feet or shoes. Georgie dropped his egg several times, but when it didn't break, he picked it up, put it back on his spoon, and ran some more. After the little boy finished the race, Allister was there to pat him on the back. "Did I win, Allister?"

"No, Georgie, but you finished. That's even more important. Good job!"

At dinner break, everyone sat on the grass and gobbled fried chicken, biscuits with butter, hard boiled eggs, fresh carrot-peas-and-lettuce salad, and rhubarb-custard pie. Two families had contributed several pails of milk to drink.

The afternoon flew by as the two Wood Lake School softball teams tried to beat each other. The game ended with the team Jim was on winning three to one.

"Let's practice this summer," Jim suggested. "Allister and I have a bat and a ball. Come to the schoolyard and we'll play some ball."

Realizing that his brother was simply trying to cheer up the members of the losing team, Allister exclaimed, "Yes, let's. But we'll have to do it in the evening—after chores."

———◆———

The last Friday of June was clean up and program practice day. When Allister and Jim came to school that morning, a list on the board assigned everyone to a team. Each team had a short list of jobs. Mr. Webster promised that the team who did the best work would get a special award that night.

Two hours later, their schoolhouse was spotless. The blackboard was clean. Chalk, eraser rags, and books rested in their places. The barrel stove was free of ash inside and wiped of soot outside. The floor was scrubbed. The windows and glass on the clock sparkled from their newspaper and vinegar rubdown. All the desks, including the teacher's, shone from a special oil rub. The outhouse seats and floor wore the scent of soap. Their usual stink below lay under a covering of stove ash. Fresh-cut pieces of old catalogues filled the toilet paper boxes. Even the stable and paddock received attention. Every brown "horse apple" was on its appointed pile at the far end of the schoolhouse acre.

When the teams had finished, Allister stood in the open schoolhouse doorway with his arms folded across his chest and a wide grin on his face. Remembering the cyclonic appearance of that very room at the end of the first day of school the previous fall, he felt complete satisfaction. *This is great. My school looks as it should!*

The final hour of the last school morning, the students stood by grade and height on the platform in front of the schoolroom to practice their recitations and songs. Mother came to play the pump organ while they sang. After practice, everyone except the teacher went home for dinner with instructions to return at 7:00 p.m., dressed in their best.

Promptly at 7:00 p.m., Mr. Webster asked his students to come up front. Allister stood next to Mabel, who looked pretty in her new white dress with its peach floral print and her blonde hair up in a French braid. Allister looked over the audience. All of the children's parents and siblings were there. He saw a young man sitting next to Mabel's parents. *I wonder who he is.*

Standing in the back row, Allister waited for his turn. As each group or student completed a song, reading, or recitation, they stepped off the stage to sit with their families.

Allister relaxed until it was Jim's turn to recite. *I helped him practice. Will he remember every word?* Allister held his breath.

Jim stepped forward. Staring at the clock on the back wall and stuffing his hands in his pockets, he recited his whole poem without hesitating:

Try, Try Again by T. H. Palmer
'Tis a lesson you should heed, if at first you don't succeed,
try, try again;
Then your courage should appear, for, if you will persevere,
You will conquer, never fear; try, try again ...

When Jim finished and went to sit with the McRuer family, Allister released his breath. *Good for him. No mistakes. Wonder if I will do as well.*

Only two students remained on the platform—Mabel and Allister. It was his turn. He gulped and stepped forward to recite the eighth chapter of the Psalms, *"O Lord, our Lord, how excellent is thy name in all the earth! who hast set thy glory above the heavens. Out of the mouth of babes and sucklings hast thou ordained strength ..."*[5]

Allister looked at his mother the whole time he was reciting. When he hesitated at the last sentence, she mouthed the first two words and he finished without stumbling. *I did it!*

As the audience clapped, Allister stepped back. He had promised to keep Mabel company while she gave the recitation that closed the program. "Recipe for a Farm Wife," she began, reciting something she had written:

Take a girl with a sturdy body that stands on faith
in her Maker.
Add a mile of smiles, a loyal heart for serving, two strong yet
gentle hands,
A pinch of wisdom to accept advice, a cup of trust to place in
her husband,

A pint of brains, a gallon of courage. Stir in home crafts
and schooling.
Pour into a close family. Bake for fifteen years at a pioneer
homestead on the prairie under the northern lights. And you
will have a farm wife.
This recipe can serve a family of eight to fifteen.

To thunderous applause and a few whistles, Mabel and Allister took their seats with their families, and the three school board members joined Mr. Webster on the platform. When their teacher called their names, the students stepped forward to receive their awards. With pride, Etta held up her Best Alphabet certificate. Amy beamed at her Best Composition. Jim looked bashfully surprised at his Best Arithmetic Scores. Etta, Nellie, and Jimmy stood together to each receive a copy of their team's Best Cleanup Crew certificate. Much to Allister's joy, he was given two prizes—one for penmanship, and another for his North American Geography projects.

"And now the most important event of the year is here," Mr. Webster said. "Wood Lake School has its very first graduate. Mabel, please come forward."

Allister glanced at Jim and slumped in the seat. *If we had remained in Quebec instead of moving here, we two would be graduating this year, just like Mabel. We had to wait for this school to be built, and I feel like I've lost a year of my life. Wonder if that delay bothers Jim as much as it does me.*

Mabel shook hands with Mr. Webster and Mr. Deacon. Standing between the two men, she held her certificate up with tears in her eyes. Applause and more whistles shook the building. Two school board members, Mr. Kempthorne and Mr. Cossar, congratulated her too.

After she made her way through the crowd, Allister saw Mabel blush when the young man standing with her parents congratulated her. *Maybe Mabel gave up on more education,* Allister thought, *because she already has a beau. But she's not quite fourteen. Here I thought Mary was too young to get married at nineteen. Well, not me. I'm finishing high school, no matter how long it takes, before I become anybody's beau.*

On the way home that evening, Father asked the twins to walk with him. "Allister, Jim, Mother and I are proud of all your hard work at school and at home. I think a fishing trip with Angus over the Dominion Day holiday will be a suitable reward, don't you?"

Both Allister and Jim jumped and yelled, "Hurray!"

A real holiday. Grinning, Allister threw an arm over his twin's shoulder. *An entire weekend with no field work or chores. We get a real holiday!*

chapter sixteen

Float Like a Boat

Chores couldn't be done fast enough to suit Allister the next morning. When he returned to the house, he asked, "Well, John, when do we leave?"

John laughed. "Got a few things to do first."

"What things?"

"Packing for one. Father is getting Shalazar and the buggy ready to take Mother and Jessie to the Dominion Day festivities in Cherry Creek, so he says we can take the wagon for our camping trip. Dan and Jim are splitting kindling to take along."

"What about me, John?" Allister asked. "What would you like me to do?"

"Get us a dozen rods for fishing poles and grilling sticks."

"Rods?"

"Yes, from the young willows growing on the shoreline of our farm's pond out beyond the barn."

"Great idea." Allister snatched one of his mother's knives and headed out the back door at a run.

John grabbed his arm. "Never run with a knife, Allister."

"Sorry, John. Just excited. Want to get going."

"Even, then …"

"Alright, alright."

When Allister returned to the farmyard, John had Jake and Maggie hitched to the wagon and was loading the food and pans Mother had provided. His tarpaulin tent that he had brought back from the stone quarry lay rolled up in the wagon bed along with the bundles of kindling and a sack of feed for the horses. After Dan had fetched an axe and a shovel, John hollered, "All aboard for the McRuers' fishing expedition."

———

"Remember Dominion Day last year, Jim?" Allister mumbled as they munched biscuits and baked chicken en route.

"Do you mean having to chase Jake and Shalazar half way to kingdom come so we could all get back home? How could I forget!"

"Well, I just hope Shalazar doesn't try to pull any stunts this year," Allister continued.

John laughed. "He'd better not, if he knows what's good for him!"

Allister tossed his chicken bone into the grass. "Say, John, you haven't told us yet where we're going."

"Pembina River near the town Killarney."

"Why that spot?"

"Because the old timers say pelicans come there every year. Where there are pelicans, there are fish."

"What are pelicans?"

"Large, white, water birds."

"Ducks?"

"No, not exactly. You'll see."

"How far away is this place?"

"A ways. We'll head north at the crossroads in the town of Wakopa."

Large white birds that fish in a river. Allister wiped his mouth with the back of his hand. *Now this I have to see.*

Even with the team trotting most of the way along the dirt wagon tracks, they didn't arrive until early evening. While Dan took care of the horses, Allister helped John and Jim set up camp among the trees not far from the river. With the tent up and a campfire blazing, John showed his brothers how to set up rocks on which to place pans above the flames. An enamel teapot full of river water was set over the embers to boil. The crackle of the burning wood, the chirr of cicadas, the buzz of a mosquito or two, and the hoot of an owl were soon the only sounds to break the stillness of the night.

At the edge of the campfire light, Jake and Maggie stood side by side, heads next to partner's tail, with drooping eyelids and one hind hoof folded under. Having eaten and drunk their fill, they were soon sound asleep. Allister chuckled. *Until tonight, I never knew a horse could snore.*

Hot oatmeal, milk, biscuits, and tea made breakfast the next morning. John cooked, Allister and Jim fed and watered the horses, and Dan cleaned up.

"Our first campout," Jim observed. "Unless you count our boxcar ride from Quebec to Manitoba."

"How did you sleep, Jim?" John asked.

"Actually better than at Will's. Dirt's a whole lot softer than boards."

"But damper," Allister complained.

"Can't have everything," Dan shrugged. "A trade off, I guess."

John dug a hole nearby and examined the soil that he turned out.

"What are you doing?" Allister asked.

"Looking for bait."

"There's one." Jim lunged and grabbed a wiggly worm.

Shoeless and with pants rolled up, the four brothers waded into the river with willow poles that dangled baited hooks from string. Allister and Jim copied John's pole movements. Dan fished with his own flourish.

There was a splash and Allister's pole bent as the hooked fish tried to make a run for it. "I've got one! What do I do now?"

"Here, hold this." John thrust his pole into Jim's hand. "Hang on, Allister. Keep the line tight."

John ran towards the end of the line and grabbed the struggling fish. Flipping it onto the shore, John stood with dripping pants looking down at Allister's catch. He picked up a rock and knocked the fish unconscious. "Allister, remove your hook and throw the fish farther up the bank. Let's catch another."

Four brothers waded once more into the river. A rustling on shore caught their attention.

"Allister, stop him!" Jim shouted. "Stop the fish thief."

It was too late. A huge white bird swallowed the panting fish with one gulp of its enormous yellow bill.

"A pelican?" Allister asked.

"Definitely. Guess we'd better hide our catch under a pan," John said.

After several hours, they had caught five fish.

"Now what?" Allister asked.

"Clean 'em." John pulled out his hunting knife. After cutting off a fish's head, he slit its belly and pulled out its guts. When he had scraped the fish's body of all its scales and washed it in the river, John handed the cleaned fish to Dan. "Skewer this onto a pair of wet willow sticks over the campfire. Now you try." John handed his knife to Allister.

Less than an hour later, the four sat around the campfire, smacking their lips on grilled fish.

"Don't know why, but when you grill your own catch, it tastes *so* much better," John sighed.

After they had cleaned up dinner dishes, John came out of the tent with his blanket. "Time for my Sunday nap. It's the day of rest, remember?"

A nap? Allister rolled his eyes. *What a way to waste a beautiful, sunny, summer holiday.*

Jim rumpled his hair and wrinkled his nose. "Suit yourself." He turned to Allister. "Let's take the horses to a place where they can graze."

Tying the tether ropes to their horses' halters as reins and pocketing two stakes, Allister and Jim found a tree stump to help them astride their giant mounts. A five minute ride took them back onto the treeless prairie. Sliding off the horses and staking the end of the tether ropes, Jim and Allister lay side by side in the grass and stared up at the blue, cloudless sky.

"We have one more year at school. What do you want to do after that?" Jim asked.

"I'd like to go to high school."

"How are you going to do that? You heard Mabel. The nearest one is in Brandon. No use dreaming. You probably can't go. Don't think Father will let you go so far for more schooling."

Allister frowned. "We'll see. The new school in Cherry Creek might be finished by the time you and I graduate from Grade 8. Maybe it will include high school. Surely Father would let me go there, if it does."

"I wouldn't bet on it if I were you," Jim grumped.

Allister thrust his hands into his pockets. *What's gotten into Jim? He's usually on my side.*

When the twins returned to their campsite a couple of hours later, Dan was fishing waist-deep in the river. John still snoozed with his shirt over his face. Jim and Allister baited their hooks and waded towards Dan. "Careful, boys," their brother warned. "There's a drop off about halfway here. I didn't expect it and swallowed a bit of water before I found my footing again."

Jim reached the drop off first. Allister grabbed his brother by the back of his pants to steady him. Seeing where Jim went down, Allister was more prepared for the large step. "Oh, boy, and none of us know how to swim."

"Maybe we should learn," Jim suggested.

"But how? Does John know, Dan?"

"Umm, not sure. Let's ask him when he wakes up."

That evening after another delicious meal of grilled fish, Dan brought up the subject of learning to swim.

"Good idea. Didn't know how myself until three weeks ago. After I turned down several invitations from the other fellas that work at the quarry, I finally went along, confessing only after we got to the local swimming hole. Flannigan showed me how to float and then crawl in the water. Did it every evening for more than a week. Refreshing way to wash off the sandstone grit."

Before breakfast the next morning, while his brothers did their own camp chores, Allister wandered among the trees along the river to gather more wood. At a point along the bank, he stopped to watch a speck on the water. When it got closer, he realized it was a rowboat. The boy in it wasn't rowing, but instead letting the boat float with the current as he fished.

Bet he catches more fish from his boat, Allister thought. *Jim and Dan might want to try it.*

Hurrying back to their campsite with his armload of sticks, Allister told his brothers what he'd seen.

"Fishing from a boat? Where would we get one?" Dan mumbled.

"Well, first things first," John said. "After cleanup, you're learning to float."

Removing shirts and shoes, the four brothers walked out past the river's drop off. John demonstrated what to do. The first time Allister tried to copy his older brother, the water went over his head and he panicked. Visions of his near-drowning their first day in Manitoba flashed through his mind. Thrashing about only made things worse. He guessed he had swallowed a gallon of the river before he saw a hand reach in to fish him out.

"Not that way." John let go when Allister finally got his feet under him. "Take a deep breath first, and then lay back slowly."

After filling his lungs with air, Allister lay in the water with arms and legs stretched out. His body bobbed on top this time. Gazing at the sky and its wisps of clouds, he relaxed.

Something with a quadruple set of narrow, transparent wings whirred nearby and a shiny, slim body with tiny feet landed on his nose. Snorting and swallowing more water, he jumped to his feet. "What was that?"

"A gorgeous dragonfly," John grinned. "No need to be afraid of it. It flies over water to catch and eat bugs."

"It thought you were a log it could rest on!" Jim chuckled. "That means you must be Bob the log."

"Bob? Where'd you get that?"

"Well, you're first name is Robert, isn't it?"

"Uh huh," Allister agreed. Lying back in the water, he relaxed and mumbled, "Bob the log ... ready for dragonfly landing."

After John was sure they knew how to float, he tried to teach his younger brothers how to do the crawl. Allister did learn to lie face down in the water and reach with cupped hands over his head to pull his body through the water. He even learned to kick with his legs out behind him. But he never got the timing for turning his head to the side to catch a breath. He always got water up his nose and in his mouth. Sputtering each time, he finally gave up. Dan and Jim caught on quickly and soon were racing John upstream.

Since he now knew how to float, Allister wondered if he could swim on his back. Trying the arm reaching and feet kicking from his usual float position, he discovered that he was swimming.

"Hey, that's a pretty good trick," John said when Allister stopped and stood up in shallow water. "You just taught yourself the backstroke."

"One problem. Couldn't see where I was going."

That afternoon as Allister, Jim, and Dan fished in another part of the river, John stuck his pole in the dirt next to their tent and hiked along the bank upstream.

"Where's he going?" Allister asked.

"He mumbled something earlier about going to find a boat for us to rent," Jim said.

Two fish and an hour later, John rowed up in a boat. "Let's try fishing from this."

Much to Allister's surprise, Jim balked. "Fishing and swimming are fun," he admitted. "But fishing from a boat?"

Allister couldn't believe his ears. *I was sure he'd be all for it.*

"With you three a long ways out on the water," Jim said, "someone needs to keep an eye on our campsite, horses, and wagon. I'll stay and fish from the shallows."

Dan and John sat shoeless and shirtless at the oars and waited for Allister to get in with poles and bait. When he was seated in the back of the boat, the two tried to row out into the middle of the river. They went around in circles at first. Watching from the shore, Jim hooted and hollered at them. Allister stifled a few chuckles and closed his eyes to keep from getting dizzy.

Coordinating their efforts finally brought real forward motion. They headed upstream, out of sight of their camp. In a short time, John and Dan caught a half dozen large fish, flipping their catch into the back of the boat near Allister's feet.

When his brothers decided they had enough fish and should return to shore, Allister asked, "John, could I take a turn at rowing?"

"Definitely."

John stood up to trade places with his brother. The boat shifted. Allister's footing was a slippery fish, and the two brothers fell into the river. Terrified in water over his head, Allister thrashed in the river until his head broke through the surface. He was too far from the boat to grab it. "Help!" He yelled. *Oh no. Not again.*

"Float, Allister," Dan hollered from the boat. "On your back."

Gulping air, Allister lay in the water and, fighting his panic, tried to relax. The current nudged his body along, causing him to drift farther from the boat. *Should I try to backstroke?* he thought. *Which direction is the river bank?*

The plopping of oars was slowly coming towards him.

Maybe Dan is going to try to rescue me.

"Dan, I'll get him." Jim's voice sounded closer than the boat's dipping oars. Out of the corner of his eye, Allister saw Maggie's head and then Jim's. With Jim on her back, the horse swam past Allister. "Grab her tail as she swims back by you," Jim said. "She can pull you towards shore."

Wisps of the mare's long, black tail floated within reach. Allister grabbed a handful and, holding onto the horse's "lifeline" with both of his hands above his head as he floated on his back, he felt Maggie draw him along the surface of the water. When his rescuers had pulled him close enough to the river bank for him to touch bottom, Allister let go.

Dripping, relieved, and grateful, he slumped on the muddy shore to catch his breath and mentally replay the amazing events. *If John hadn't taught me to float … If Jim hadn't known that horses can swim … I wouldn't be …*

Allister stood up. *John! He fell in the water, too.* With his heart in his throat, Allister scanned the river. No John. Turning to look along the shore, relief flooded Allister once more. John was walking toward him. *He must have swum to the bank.*

By the time the "dunked" arrived back at camp, Dan had rowed the boat to their campsite and unloaded fish and poles. Horse and rider stood nearby, dripping and puffing.

"Thanks for saving my life." Allister slapped Jim on his back.

"Thank Maggie," Jim said. "She's the rescue swimmer."

Allister ran his hand down the horse's white blaze and reached up to pat her wet neck. "Good girl, Maggie. Thank you."

Maggie nudged Allister's arm with her muzzle, as if to say, "You're welcome!"

"Guess we've had enough excitement for one day," John said. "Go ahead with the cleaning and cooking of our catch. I need to get the boat back to its owner."

The next day, the four brothers landed one more batch of fish. After putting them alive in buckets of river water to take home to Mother, Allister helped his brothers break camp.

"We're taking a different route home, boys." Dan drove the team north over a bridge and through Killarney. At the crossroads in town, he headed west.

Allister grew more puzzled. "Where are you taking us?"

Dan turned in the seat and smiled. "Wait and see."

Several hours later, he directed the team onto a well-worn trail leading south.

"Dan, this can't be the trail we took to the campsite," Allister said.

"You're right, Allister. It isn't."

When Dan left the trail and had the team go cross-country along a stream bank, Allister complained, "Where in the world are you taking us? This ground is so bumpy, we're soon going to slosh all of the water out of our buckets."

"Not to worry. There's the creek if we need more water." Dan pointed at the rivulet of water. "Allister, I'm asking you to be a little more patient. I have a surprise to show you."

After skirting farm fields for another six miles, Dan reined in the team. Turning in the driver's seat, he gestured at the grassy spans around the wagon and asked, "Well, what do you think of it?"

Allister scanned their surroundings. *What is this place? There's nothing here.*

chapter seventeen

The Stone School

Staring at the wide expanse of prairie around him, Jim shrugged and asked, "Think about what?"

"This claim. Joe told me it's available," Dan said. "John, help me find its stakes. Joe said I'll need to know the number painted on them when I go to register for this section."

Dan and John threaded through the waist-high stems, sweeping the grass aside with their arms and looking for a small stake. Finding one, they walked west to search for the second.

When their brothers disappeared from sight, Jim jumped down from the back of the wagon. "Might as well let the horses graze. Looks like we'll be here a while."

Allister climbed down and unhitched Maggie. While he stood next to his father's four-legged grass mower, he felt a familiar dread creep over him. *Dan is leaving, too. If this departure goes anything like Will's, I won't be able to pass my exams and graduate from Grade 8, let alone complete the next school year.*

"Alright, we found all four of them." Dan's voice cut through Allister's reverie. "The centre of the land I hope to claim is right about here." Dan moved off a few dozen yards.

Jim led Jake next to Dan and looked around. "Any water nearby?"

"Not really. Local creek's about a mile and a half that way." Dan pointed.

"Neighbours not too far away," John said. "Good grass for livestock."

"But no broken sod, no fencing, no buildings, and no well," Allister added, voicing his anxiety. "From scratch. Again!"

"Don't worry, little brother." Dan walked over and put his hand on Allister's shoulder. "I won't let Father pull you boys out of school to help me with my claim."

"Thanks, Dan. I really want to finish the eighth grade, at the very least. It was extremely difficult to finish seventh last year—because of all the school we missed."

"I know. Saw you burn the late-night kerosene and study on weekends."

Back in the wagon, Allister asked, "How far is this claim from Mary and Joe's homestead? How far is it from ours?"

"Several miles from Mary and Joe's. A little over one from home."

"Then you could live at home while you work on your claim."

"That's the plan."

"He'll get more help from me, too," John added, grinning, "once I'm done with the quarry work."

"When do you go back to work, John?" Allister asked.

"At dawn."

When John, Jim, and Allister brought the buckets with the fish into the house, Mother didn't look exactly pleased. "How long have these fish been out of water?"

"They haven't," John said. "Kept them alive in the buckets."

Mother peered into the buckets. "Well, I don't mind cooking the fish, but I don't like cleaning them. You caught 'em. You clean 'em."

Depositing his bucket next to the wood pile, John sat on a stump and with a grumble or two set to gut and scrape the fish. Dan handed Allister and Jim two knives. "Help your brother. I'll take care of the horses."

Later, Allister stayed in the kitchen while Mother fixed the fish, because he had a few questions he wanted to ask. After fetching canned tomatoes from the cellar, and lettuce and radishes from the garden, he watched her bread the fish. While the fish lay in bubbling butter in the hot frying pan, Allister asked, "Mother, did Dan ever talk to you about getting his own claim?"

"Yes. When you boys were at Will's."

"Did he seem to have a specific claim in mind then?"

"No."

"Did you give him any advice about picking a claim?"

"Guess I did. I pointed out that it'd be harder for us to help him and impossible to share animals or machinery with him if he claimed one far away, like Will did. Why?"

"Because on our way home today, Dan drove us cross-country to an open claim. It's not far, about a mile, part way between here and Joe's."

Allister looked up to see the biggest smile spread across his mother's tired face, and tears well up in her eyes. "Thanks for telling me, Allister."

The back door opened and slammed shut.

"Chickens in," Jessie said, putting a handful of eggs in a basket. "Oh, Allister, you miss big sad ... chicks get out. Run away. Next thing ... yellow fluff in grass ... behind grain shed. On Sunday ... we get home from Dominion party ... a red and white dog have Mathilda in his mouth. He's gone. He took Mathilda!"

Mathilda? Allister thought. *Oh, no. That was Jessie's favourite hen. Red and white dog? Must have been a fox.* He squatted so he could look his little sister in the eye. "I'm so sorry. She was your favourite, wasn't she? Hmm. Sounds like we need to teach a fox some manners."

"The dog wasn't a dog? It was a ..."

"A fox, Jessie. Fox."

"F ... fox?" she asked. When Allister nodded, she spouted. "Fox! I hate him! Poor Mathilda!"

"Tomorrow Jim and I'll fix the fence so the chicks can't get out, alright?"

"Oh, thank you," Jessie said, wrapping her arms around Allister's neck, "Glad you're home. I miss you."

At supper, Allister bit into the crisp coating of Mother's fried fish. Although the grilled fish on their camping trip had tasted good, he much preferred this.

"Mother, when did Father leave for Cherry Creek?" John asked.

"He didn't return home with Jessie and me. Stayed in town. But he made sure that Jessie and I still had a horse and buggy to take us home after our fun on Dominion Day." Mother laughed. "Neither of us wanted a repeat of what happened last year."

"So Shalazar stayed put?" Allister asked.

"Your father made sure of it. He boarded my horse at the livery stable for the day. Shalazar was locked up in a sturdy paddock until we went to get him."

"Well, boys, time for evening chores," John said. "Good supper, Mother. Thanks."

"You're welcome. Sorry to be grumpy about the fish earlier," Mother said. "They were a special treat. Thanks for bringing them home. I do love to eat them, but really don't like to clean them!"

"Alright, Mother. We'll make a bargain with you. We catch and clean. You cook. We all enjoy." Grinning widely, Dan gave Mother a peck on her cheek.

Outside, the brothers scattered. Allister and Jim walked to the south pasture to get the cattle. Opening the gate and whistling into the semi-darkness, Allister didn't have long to wait. Bessie must have been standing close by, because she and her calf made straight for the barn. Soon five Angus cows with calves followed with the herd's bull plodding at the rear. As their animals filed into the barn, Allister stood for a moment to watch the lingering twilight. Manitoba's sunsets seemed to have more shades of leftover sunglow than he'd ever been able to count. Three dark shapes stood side by side in the pasture not far away. *Dan must have turned the horses out together to graze.*

———————

The next morning, Dan had taken John in the buggy by the time Allister, Jim, and Jessie went outside to do morning chores. Just as they finished, Dan drove up and put Shalazar in the south pasture with the rest of their livestock.

With Father and John doing stonework, and Will farming his own claim, Allister's next oldest brother, Dan, was now in charge. His method of "being-in-charge" was a bit confusing to Allister at first. Each morning, Dan would leave the house without giving either Allister or Jim any instructions. At the end of each day during supper, Dan would ask what everybody had done and what they thought should be done next. The absence of Father's step-by-step directions seemed to bother Jim the most. He appeared to not know what to do or when to do it.

Allister, on the other hand, caught on quickly. Farm life as he knew it had daily and weekly routines and seasonal rhythms. When Dan and Jake returned from Turtle Mountain dragging a log, Allister begged Jim to help him saw, split, and stack it. During the hot, dry days, Allister wheedled Jim into helping water both Mother's and the schoolyard's trees. In her garden, Mother persuaded Jim to help Allister water, pull weeds, and gather fresh vegetables for their summer suppers. July was hay month. Several days after Dan drove the mower over the fields, Allister took turns with Jim driving the dump rake to turn the drying hay. Then the three mounded it into the barn loft. When that was full, they made outdoor stacks.

Essentially his own boss during daylight hours, Allister paced himself. He'd finish the necessary work and still have time to read a number of the books he'd borrowed from the school's bookcase, which he accessed with Mother's key.

Whenever Allister could talk Jim into working as a team, there was always time for the evening softball practice that Jim had promised his Wood Lake schoolmates.

———

After the three brothers had put up the first batch of hay, Allister decided he had waited long enough. *Have to see for myself how the stone schoolhouse in Cherry Creek is progressing. Will the building be ready this fall, or sometime later? Will the new school have just Grades 1 through 8, or will it include Grades 9 through 11, too? Cherry Creek is much closer than Brandon. If the new schoolhouse has a high school, my chances of getting some high school will be better.*

One Saturday after chores and breakfast, Allister begged Mother to take him to town with her on her usual trip to Cherry Creek. "That's a good idea," she said. "Jim, do you want to come, too?"

"Yep. Work's caught up for now."

"I'll stay here and guard Jessie's chickens," Dan said, grabbing a broom and pretending to chase a fox.

Jessie burst into giggles. "Then we ..." she said, counting on her fingers, "four go."

"Jim, be sure to bring along a halter and two lead ropes when you hitch up Shalazar," Mother said. "We'll double tie him every time we stop."

When Jim drove the buggy to the back door, Allister stood in front of Shalazar. He held the horse's head firmly while Jim lifted Jessie in, handed Mother up, and loaded the picnic basket, sale items, and sacks of grain in the back of the buggy. Shalazar threw his head up and acted like he wanted to run. Allister hung on, yelling, "Whoa!"

Jim came around to check on the horse. Tightening the bridle's chin strap, he said, "Wait 'til I have him well in hand before you let go. He's acting like the bit of a dickens today. Guess he knows he's being handled by two boys."

"Here, give me those reins," Mother said, looking grim. "Shalazar, stop that! Whoa!" She pulled hard on the mouth of the mettlesome horse. Shalazar lowered his head. Still chomping on the bit, he finally stood quietly.

Hmm, Allister thought. *This horse has finally recognized his mistress. Good going, Mother!*

Shalazar made short work of the twelve miles between home and town. First stop was the gristmill. Putting Shalazar's halter on over his bridle, Mother tied him with two lead ropes to the hitching rail in front of the mill. "Alright, I think he'll stay put. Let's do our trade first. Father's dinner break isn't until noon. We'll go see him then."

Allister and Jim helped her carry two sacks of wheat and one of oats into the mill's office. After Jessie had picked out a flour-sacking print she liked, Mother made arrangements to collect the flour and rolled oats later that afternoon. Directing her horse to the hitching rail in front of Nicol's General Store, she said, "One more stop before we see Father."

Although his mother and oldest brother, John, had come numerous times for delivery of goods or on supply runs, it'd been a year since Allister had been in town. He entered the store expecting a few surprises and wasn't disappointed. There were baskets of berries and cans of salmon from other parts of Canada. A sign said a shipment of pears and apples would also be arriving soon. A bicycle rested in a corner. Replacement parts for bicycles, and pumps for tires, crowded shelves. New styles of shoes, dresses, shirts, pants, and hats were on display. Dolls in pretty dresses were among the toys in a glass case. Allister, Jim, and Jessie had gotten their eyes full by the time Mother finished her shopping.

Jessie grabbed her mother's hand and dragged her over to the jars of candy that sat on one counter. Pointing at the jar with her favourite sweet, lemon drops, she begged. "Mother, one piece, please."

"Not now, Jessie. We haven't eaten our picnic dinner yet. Here, children, help me carry out these items."

Hefting a bag of sugar on one shoulder, Allister gathered bundles of fabric under the other arm. While he, Jim, and Jessie were carrying Mother's purchases out to the wagon, Allister saw his mother buy several pieces of candy and hide them in the pocket of her skirt.

Once they had loaded everything, Mother drove their buggy down a side street, past a familiar line of trees. Turning off the street, she directed Shalazar across the schoolyard. Allister looked up at the stone structure that rose behind the two-room school. In comparison, the new school was huge.

As the McRuer's buggy rounded the new building, Allister saw a man bending over a large piece of rock. He was pounding chips away with a chisel and a wooden mallet. At the approach of the horse and buggy, the mason stood up. It was Father. "Well, hello, family," he said, smiling through a layer of sandstone dust. "Come to take me to dinner, eh?"

A school bell rang from the other side of the building. Men climbed down ladders and walked different directions, some carrying dinner pails. Father clapped his hands and laughed. A cloud of dust rose from them and disbursed in the prairie breeze. "Be back in a moment." When he came back, his face and hands were clean.

Picking up a mallet and a wooden stake and saying, "Follow me," Father ambled to the edge of town and into the prairie grass. Standing next to the buggy and taking the reins from Mother, he said, "This should do. Let's have our picnic here."

"Great spot." Mother smiled, climbed down, and gave her husband a hug, murmuring, "I've missed you."

"Catch me, Father." Without giving him much time to get ready, Jessie jumped from the buggy. But he caught her and swung her up on his shoulders. She squealed in delight, not seeming to notice the cloud of dust that rose from his clothes.

"Here, Allister. Pound this stake into the ground over there," Father pointed. "Jim, you unhitch Shalazar and tether him to the stake so he can graze while we eat our dinner."

Mother set down her picnic basket. Kneeling in the grass, she passed out fried chicken, fresh lettuce and carrots, biscuits, oatmeal cookies, and slices of rhubarb pie. From the back of the buggy, Jim lifted out the jug of cold tea. Mother gave everyone a tin cup to help themselves. When she handed Father his cup, she said, "This was Allister's idea."

"It was?" Father appeared surprised. "Now, Allister, be honest. Which did you want to see most—the new school or me?"

"Both, Father. The new school looks wonderful. And we're really happy to see you!"

Father laughed.

"We miss you." Jessie hugged her father. "A fox get Mathilda. John cut some fish. Allister almost drown. Dan find a stake. They make hay."

"Whoa! Whoa!" Father held up his hands in objection. "One story at a time. Start by telling me what happened to Mathilda, Jessie."

Allister groaned and rolled his eyes. *The dinner hour is going by far too quickly. There won't be enough time after all of Jessie's stories for me to find out what I need to know.* Exasperated, he interrupted his sister's story about John's cleaning of the fish to blurt his burning question. "Father, how many grades will be offered in the new school?"

"All eleven, as soon as they can find teachers qualified to teach high school."

A huge smile grew on Allister's face. *High school will no longer be seventy miles away in Brandon*, he thought. *Now I'm glad to be without a father and my big brother all this time.* But all he said out loud was, "That's great, Father!"

"When are you coming home?" Mother asked.

"In about three weeks. Almost finished with the stonework. A lot of other construction needs to done, but I've already put my boss on notice that I must return home. Harvest season is right around the corner. The oats should almost be ready. Mother, better remind Dan to check the reaper's blades. They may need sharpening."

Mother packed up the dinner basket. Father hitched up Shalazar and kept a firm grip on the reins. "Allister and Jim, help Jessie into the buggy and then get in yourselves. Mother, walk with me a bit."

"In a minute." Mother reached into her skirt's pocket.

Allister laughed. "I wondered when you were going to hand out those lemon drops."

"Lemon drops?" Jessie almost fell out of the buggy, reaching for them.

Allister grabbed his sister by the waist. "Jessie, sit down. Don't worry, Mother will give you one."

To the sounds of Jessie's loud slurping and the swish of the tall grass as his parents and Shalazar moved towards the stone school, Allister strained to listen to his parents' murmuring conversation. He couldn't make out what they were saying. As they approached the building, Allister could see that only a few stones were missing from the back gable and the top of the chimney. The school's two-storey, stone shell was almost complete. He felt his dreams rise with the height of its walls. *I hope I'll get the chance to walk its hallways as one of its students.*

<hr />

Almost a week after their visit with Father, Allister saw John walk across the oat field to the reaper. Allister and Jim stopped what they were doing and ran over to welcome their oldest brother home. Since it was late afternoon and Dan was only two acres short of having all the oats cut and bundled, John encouraged them to finish their task first. He reminded them there would be plenty of time for catch-up stories later. Giving up his seat on the binder to John, Dan helped Allister and Jim lift and lean the oat bundles against each other in rows of golden pyramids called stooks. At nightfall, Allister and his twin herded the livestock from the south pasture to the barn. John and Dan unhitched the team and rode them back to their stalls and grain dinner.

———◆———

"Let's go to Deloraine today," John said to Dan at breakfast the following Monday. "Allister, Jim, you can come too."

"What's at Deloraine?" Allister asked.

"You'll see."

chapter eighteen

The Claims

"John, how long will this trip to Deloraine take?" Allister asked from his perch in the wagon bed on his brother's rolled up tent.

"Only three days," John said. "Mother and Jessie promised to do the chores while we're gone."

Acting as if they were delighted at the lighter load, Jake and Maggie trotted much of the way. Near the town of Cherry Creek, they turned west onto a well-worn dirt road.

Several miles along, Allister saw more and more birds flying above them. There seemed to be hundreds, some flocks circling, many heading south. He couldn't believe the ruckus the birds were making. Their calls to each other almost drowned out conversation. "Why are there so many birds above this part of the trail, John?"

"We're getting close to the marsh around Whitewater Lake," John explained. "Maybe we should've combined this trip with some hunting."

"Better we didn't," Dan said. "Father isn't home from his masonry work on the new school yet. We shouldn't leave Mother and Jessie too long."

The variety of plumed aviators is nothing short of a wonder, Allister thought. He hollered to be heard above the din, "John, do you know the names of any of these fliers?"

John pulled up the team. Pointing at each group above them, he called out, "Canadian geese, mallard ducks, blue herons, egrets, whooping cranes, sandhill cranes, gulls, snow geese, pin-tail ducks, red-wing blackbirds."

"How do you know all their names?" Jim yelled.

"An older timer told Will and me last fall when we were hunting."

"No pelicans," Allister observed.

"No, because it has no fish," John said. "This marshy lake has no outlet. Creeks flow into it, but nothing flows out. Some years, it dries up."

They rode on, later rolling through a small town.

"Not Deloraine?" Dan asked.

"No, Whitewater," Allister said. "I saw a sign."

Allister and his three brothers gradually passed the marsh and left its noisy guests and residents behind. They crossed railroad tracks, rolled over a creek, and through a second small town.

A short way past the second town, John stopped the team on the bank of another stream. "We'll camp here."

That night, Allister was glad enough to pull the tent flaps tight. The Whitewater marsh was not only a sanctuary for thousands of birds, but also ten times that number of mosquitoes. In addition, the cool bite of the first fall breeze was blowing.

Midmorning the next day, Allister got his first look at Deloraine. Like Cherry Creek, it had a collection of businesses and houses, a train depot, and a grain elevator. It, too, was a relatively new "plant" springing from the prairie. Unlike its neighbouring towns farther up the tracks, however, Deloraine was the end of the line. Trains arrived from and left towards the east.

John drove down the main street. "Keep a sharp eye now. We're looking for the land office."

Ah, a place for filing homestead claims, Allister thought. *That's why we're here. I remember Father mentioning such an office in one of his letters when he first came to Manitoba four years ago.*

"Stop!" Hollering to be heard above the din of the busy town, Allister pointed down a side street. "I saw a sign—that way."

Carts, buggies, and wagons clogged the street in front of the land office. Half a block away, John set the wagon brake and Dan, Jim, and Allister followed him into the agency. Plenty of men were milling about, looking at survey charts. Since John and Dan knew exactly which sites they wanted, they approached the only clerk who wasn't busy at the moment. Introducing themselves to the young man, they pulled slips of paper out of their pockets on which they had written the numbers from the corner stakes of the sections of land they wished to claim.

"One moment please," the clerk said. "There might be a problem with the claim Dan wants."

Will he have to select a different one? I wonder what the problem is. Allister watched the young man thumb through papers from a filing cabinet and talk to another agent.

When the clerk returned to the counter, he said, "You're in luck, Dan. Another fellow was in here two days ago asking about that same property. He wasn't able to file a claim on it, though, because he didn't have enough money for the fee. How much of this claim are you filing for?"

"Only the western section, because twenty dollars is all the money I have," Dan said.

"I could lend you some," John offered.

"No thanks. Three hundred twenty acres is plenty to start with."

"How many acres are you filing for, John?" Allister asked.

"All six hundred forty of it."

Elbowing between his older brothers, Jim asked, "Where is it?"

John pointed to the square on the chart. Moving his finger one square over, he said, "Father's."

"Right next door?" Allister and Jim chimed at the same time.

"Exactly."

"How many McRuers are there?" the older agent asked. "So far we have four McRuer claims in this part of Manitoba."

John laughed. "And that's probably not the end yet."

Allister folded his arms across his chest and frowned. *He's guessing Jim and I'll put our names on claims when we're old enough. Jim, probably. Me? Maybe not.*

While John and Dan completed the filing process, Allister walked along the counter, watching the other clerks work with their files, papers, and charts. *I wonder what it'd be like to work in such an office,* he thought. *It looks a whole lot more interesting than haying.*

Back in the street, John and Dan showed off the signed copies of their claims.

"Doesn't a claim mean that you don't own the land outright, yet?" Allister asked.

"That's right, little brother," Dan said.

"Then what do you have to do to own it completely?"

"The agent told us that we have three years to make improvements on the land."

"Did the man mention what kind?"

"Dig a well. Construct buildings. Plow acreage that produces a crop," John said.

"Plant trees. Set up permanent fencing. Live on the property," Dan added.

"Exactly. That, too."

"How will the agent know that you've done any of that?" Allister asked.

"They probably send someone out from the office to check. To see with their own eyes," John said as they all climbed back into the wagon. "Let's get some dinner at a hotel restaurant. My treat."

By late afternoon, the McRuer brothers had retraced much of the road between Deloraine and Cherry Creek. Over the bobbing heads of their horses, Allister could see the road crossed one more stream.

"This is Barton's Creek," John said. "Let's camp here. We're about halfway home."

John turned the team south along the creek and stopped them about half a mile from the road. Long before the sunset, the four brothers were sitting around a campfire, eating reheated beef stew from Mother's canning jars, some slices of bread and cheese they had bought in Deloraine, and drinking hot tea.

With the fading of the twilight came the onslaught of mosquitoes. Swatting at several, Allister complained, "These pests seem extra-anxious lately."

"That's probably because they know they'll be dead soon," John said. "The air tonight has an extra chill to it. Jake and Maggie are already growing their winter coats. Wouldn't be surprised if we have an early frost this year."

Once home, John's bossiness irritated Allister. *From the way he's constantly after us, he's acting as if it's going to snow next week. But it's only August. What's the matter with him?*

Before Father got home, the McRuer brothers brought in another crop of hay and piled up cordwood both at home and the schoolhouse. While Allister and Jim helped Mother harvest the tomatoes from her garden, John and Dan started a well shaft on Dan's claim.

As he had promised, Father returned home on a mid-August Friday night. At his insistence, the family began the wheat harvest the very next morning and didn't stop for Sunday that year. Mother and Jessie went to worship service by themselves. Allister wasn't happy about spending the "day of rest" in the fields, but with Father and John back, Allister was no longer his own boss.

Thirty acres and three days short of completing their harvest, Allister stumbled outside in the morning to see frost on plants along the path to the outhouse. John had been right. The first fall frost was weeks early.

"Good thing you've already got the tomatoes in, Mother," Father said at breakfast. "The twins can help you this morning with the most urgent garden work, but after dinner, I'll need everyone in the fields 'til sundown."

Allister looked longingly out the kitchen window at the schoolhouse that stood empty on the other side of his father's pasture fence. *Dig, bend, carry. Bend, lift, stack. There seems no end to it. Oh, for time to read a book! I'd rather work my brain than my body. I can't wait for school to start again.*

When the older brothers headed for the fields, Mother handed Jim and Allister a shovel, a trowel, and several bushel baskets. "Harvest the sweet corn first," she said. "Find a scythe and cut down the corn stalks. Feed the stalks to Bessie. Then dig up all the carrots and onions, rub them clean, and put them in the cellar. Jessie and I are going to can tomatoes this morning. Help us when you finish. We'll work on the potatoes another day."

When Allister and Jim entered the kitchen with the last of the carrots midmorning, Jessie and Mother were up to their elbows in tomato skins. Washed canning jars lined the top of the table. One set of processed jars was already on the table under some towels so they would cool slowly.

"Allister, Jim, you're just in time. Allister, after you put those in the cellar, I need some more firewood chopped and the stove stoked. Jim, give your hands and arms a good scrubbing. I need help stuffing the skinned tomatoes in some jars. Allister, when you're finished with the stove, wash your hands too. You and Jessie can shuck the corn."

"Alright, but I want to open a few windows first," Jim complained. "It's hotter than Hades in here."

"Umm … just a little, if it's not windy," Mother laughed. "Guess we're use to the steamy heat from the kettles, but a little fresh air wouldn't hurt. First frost means there are few flies to worry us now."

As Jim moved from window to window around the kitchen, Allister murmured, "I wonder what Mary's doing now."

"Probably harvesting vegetables from her own garden. Miss her, don't you, Allister?" Mother said.

He nodded and headed out the door to split the kindling. As he walked towards the back door with an armload, he saw a horse and buggy pull up next to the schoolhouse. Allister paused to watch a man help a woman down from the buggy and unlock the door for her. *That's right. I don't have long to wait, after all. The school year will begin again in five days. Unfortunately, none of my family has been available to help clean the school or whitewash the outhouses. Other volunteers did those chores this summer.*

Allister thought about the drive through the small town of Desford on the way back from the land office in Deloraine those weeks ago. A new building was in progress. News his mother brought home from church included information about the building—a one-room schoolhouse. He was glad the children from the farms around Desford would have a chance for an education.

At Wood Lake School last year, the teacher had been a young man who managed to complete the year, even though it was obvious to Allister that the teacher had little training and no experience with little children or beginners. Allister remembered hearing that Mr. Webster had given up teaching. *The man probably found it harder than he thought it would be.*

"Allister, what are you looking at?" Jim's voice came through an open window.

"The new teacher. I think our new teacher is a she!" Allister couldn't help thinking, *Oh boy, this year, school is guaranteed to be worse than last year.*

chapter nineteen

Miss French

"Better hustle, Allister," Mother said when he bounded down the stairs into the kitchen Monday morning. "Breakfast will be ready soon. Don't forget you have chores to do before we eat."

After a quick trip to the outhouse, Allister ran for the barn with Jim right behind him. When they finished their chores, they went back to the house, ate breakfast with Jessie and Mother, and got ready for the first day of school. In answer to her daughter's pleading, Mother had finally said Jessie could attend school with Allister and Jim. To help the new teacher and Jessie, Mother said she would come, too.

Standing around the schoolyard were seventeen students. When Allister, Jim, Jessie, and Mother arrived, Georgie ran up to Jim. "Tag. You're it!"

All the students from last year ran madly in every direction. Three new ones stood for a moment and then ran too. The game was on. Jessie stood in front of the school, watching. A girl who had become "it" saw Jessie and tagged her. Jessie laughed at being included, but could only stumble clumsily after a retreating child. Allister ran near his sister, let her touch him, and then continued the mad chasing. On impulse, Allister tagged his mother. Startled, she stared at her son and then joined the game, laughing as she ran.

The lively high-jinx came to a screeching halt when the teacher came out of the schoolhouse with a bell in one hand and a folded flag in the other. Allister stood and studied her every move. *Here begins another bad first day of a school year. When a man like Mr. Webster can fail as a teacher, how can this teacher do any better? She's a girl. My guess? Just a little older than me. Oh boy, more chaos. How will I learn anything! And I have to pass my exams at the end of the school year to graduate from Grade 8! Oh boy, oh boy.*

A few of the children stopped running and gathered around the young woman while she rang the bell. "Good morning, children," she called loudly, drawing two imaginary lines with her hand. "Please line up, boys here, and girls here. Quiet please! We'll do our opening exercises outside after this young man helps me put up the flag." She walked over to James and handed him the flag.

Two girls started to whisper, but the teacher turned immediately and demanded quiet. When the flag was raised, the teacher led the singing of "God Save the Queen" and the recitation of the Lord's Prayer. "Now, girls, you may go in. Sit on the right side of the room. No talking!'

As they filed in, Mother walked up to the teacher and introduced herself. "Hello, I'm Mrs. McRuer, Jessie's mother. Although Jessie's seven, she's never attended school before. I'm here today to help her."

"Thank you, Mrs. McRuer. Welcome to my class," the teacher said. "Now, boys, enter quietly and sit on the left side of the room."

When Allister entered the room, he noticed a few changes. Above the front blackboard, a picture of Queen Victoria hung. Below the picture lay a colourful braided rug on the platform. Between the windows on the right was a second blackboard. On all of the window ledges sat potted plants. Along the wall to the left of the door hung a large, blank square of corkboard in a wooden frame. *Potted plants and a rug in a prairie school?* Allister thought. *Looks like someone's sitting room in town!*

"Good morning, children. I'm your new teacher. My name is Miss French. I'm from Wassewa, a small town not far from here."

While Miss French talked with pride about her pioneer homesteading family, Allister studied his new teacher. No taller than his mother with dark brown eyes, and black hair that hung part way down her back in a doubled up braid, Miss French looked like she couldn't be a day over sixteen. Dressed in a light-grey blouse with a white lace collar and a long, full, black skirt, the young woman made a pretty schoolmarm.

154

"And now it's your turn to introduce yourself to me, one at a time. Stand next to your desk. Say your name, your age, your birth date, your grade in school if you know it, and your hobby, your favourite thing to do. Our oldest girl goes first."

When the children introduced themselves, some of them couldn't think of a hobby. Many stated a favourite chore, but Miss French insisted on a favourite game or fun activity. While Allister listened, he realized for the first time that everyone's childhood had been filled with work—just like his had been. Unlike many of them, however, he had one genuine hobby—reading. More recently, he had discovered two more—studying the Bible and fishing, as long as fishing didn't include swimming. He shuddered when he thought of his near-drowning in the Pembina River last summer.

When it was Jessie's turn, Mother had to prompt her to say each item.

"Name ... Jessie. I ... seven. My birthday ... July ..."

"Jessie, what do you like to do?" Mother asked.

"Mathilda!" With that, Jessie sat down, refusing to say more.

"Mathilda was Jessie's favourite chicken," Mother explained. "That hen used to follow Jessie everywhere and eat feed from her hand."

"Jessie, where is Mathilda now?" Miss French asked.

"Fox!" Jessie said. Then she pouted with her arms folded across her chest.

"Oh no," a few children mumbled with sympathy.

"That's too bad," Miss French echoed. Looking at the other children, she added, "A fox got one of your chickens too, didn't he?"

Some of the children nodded their heads.

After the introductions, Allister looked thoughtfully at the oldest new student, Sammy Le Feete. *He's my age, but he's in the first grade. This is going to be a tough year for him and Miss French.*

Next, the teacher pointed at rules she had written on a big piece of butcher paper. While she went over each rule, Miss French made it very clear that she wasn't going to put up with any nonsense. "One more thing ... there are two outhouse passes hanging from the bulletin board near the door. When you need to go, don't ask me. Just take a pass. Hang it up when you get back. There is one for boys and one for girls. If the proper pass isn't there when you want to go, you must wait your turn."

On the board, the teacher had written the agenda for the day. The first three activities were completed—opening exercises, introductions, and school rules. Reading was the next subject.

Miss French called Allister and Jim to her desk. She handed them their reading books, a dictionary, and two copies of their assignment. "The first assignment is an overview of your new text. You need to know certain vocabulary before you can answer some of the questions, so use the dictionary. Jim, please look up the word 'character.'"

Keeping a wary eye on the rest of her students, Miss French waited. When Jim had trouble finding it, she showed him how to use the guide words at the top of each page to help him speed up his search. "Alright, Jim, you do the vocabulary work first."

After she had sent Allister and Jim back to their seats, Miss French called up the students one grade at a time until all except the first graders had their assignments. When it was the first graders' turn, the teacher asked them to sit on the rug at her feet while the tall boys, James and Sammy, sat on the recitation bench nearby.

Although Allister pretended to be doing his work, he paid more attention to what was going on in front of the room. *I watched Mr. Webster, our teacher last year, fail with beginners. I wonder how Miss French will do.*

"Children, Jessie just told us about a special chicken, Mathilda," the teacher said. "Have any of you had a special chicken like Mathilda? Remember the rule, now. Raise your hand. Stand when I call your name. Then answer the question. Yes, Etta?"

"We had a chick named Hattie. Hattie turned out to be a rooster, not a hen."

Miss French chuckled.

"When Hattie got a little older," Etta added, "Mother made him into chicken with dumplings."

"Etta, why did your mother make Hattie into chicken and dumplings?"

"Because Hattie was a rooster and roosters can't lay eggs."

"So your mother wanted eggs?"

Etta nodded and sat down.

"Like this one?" the teacher asked, pulling an egg out of her pocket. She handed the egg to the child closest to her. "Pass it around. Take a good look at it. What do you see?"

One at a time the children stood and said one thing about the egg when the teacher called their names.

"It's round."

"It has a hard shell."

"It's not round. Mother says it's oval. That's right, isn't it, Miss French?"

"It's white on the outside."

"It's yellow on the inside."

"A baby chick comes out of it after a hen lays it and sits on it a great while."

"Very good, children," Miss French said. "You know a lot about eggs. You were right to say the egg is oval." The teacher picked up a piece of chalk and drew two shapes on the board. "Which one is the egg shape? Show me, Sammy. That's right. James, what is the name of the other shape?"

"A circle, Miss French."

"That's correct, James. Georgie, can you find another circle in the room? Here's my pointer. Can you show us?"

All of the first grade students looked eagerly around the room. Several pointed and whispered.

"Be quiet," Miss French demanded. "Give Georgie time to find the shape."

Allister gave up his pretense of doing his own work. He sat with elbows on his book and chin in his hands. *This teacher is so patient ... and thorough.* A wide grin spread across his face.

Georgie stood holding the pointer, looking at everything in the room. With a big smile, the small boy walked over to the clock hanging on the wall and pointed at its round face.

"Very good. That's right." The teacher drew something else on the blackboard. "What shape is this? Yes, James?"

"It isn't a shape. It's a line ... a straight line."

"That's right. We use many straight lines to write the letters of the alphabet, like this letter—E." Out of her pocket, Miss French pulled a card with the capital letter on it. "When you write some alphabet letters a little later, I want you to think about the egg. When we spell 'egg,' the very first letter of the word is E."

Next, Miss French picked up a picture she had drawn. "What's this?"

The children were quiet as they studied the drawing.

"Yes, Emily?"

"A farm."

"James, can you tell us some things on a farm?"

Allister was amazed as he watched and listened to the progression of the lesson. Before it was finished, Miss French had taught the first graders the capital forms of the letters E, F, H, and T, with a familiar word for each letter. At the same time, during the discussion about each word, the teacher introduced a few new words. *Miss French has to be a brand new teacher because of her age*, Allister thought, *but she's great. I'm going to learn a lot this year!*

When she finished the lesson, she sent seven of the children back to their seats with slates and pieces of chalk to practice the four letters. After calling Allister to her desk, the teacher assigned him to help the seated first graders with their four capital letters. She also told Allister that when the first graders who were returning students were ready, he could help them practice the small case of each of the four letters and perhaps spell the word that went with each of those letters. "You have the very best penmanship, so ask for their best too," Miss French instructed Allister. "Sammy will probably need the most help. Your mother will help Jessie."

Then Miss French called up Jim. His assignment was to help the rest of the first graders at the board on the side wall. "Since Henry and Violet are new students, they'll need the most help," she said. "They should practice only the capitals."

"Teena and John, please come sit on the rug with your readers," the teacher called.

After Miss French had taught the reading lessons to the second and the fifth graders, she asked them to help the first graders draw a picture of each word for the alphabet letters, an egg, a farm, a hat, a table. While the rest of their schoolmates were busy drawing, the teacher called Jim and Allister to the front. Sitting on the rug cross-legged with small lap desks across their knees, the twins worked with Miss French on their reading assignment and started arithmetic before they went back to their seats.

"Everyone, look," she instructed as she stood up with her hand raised. "When you see my hand up, you stop what you're doing and you close your mouth, which means no whispers even, and you raise your hand too. When everyone has done that, you'll all be ready to listen to me. It's now time for your fifteen minutes of recess. The quietest row will be dismissed first."

All rustling stopped. Each completely quiet row was dismissed, one at a time.

Recess sounded louder than Allister remembered. All twenty students seemed to have bottled up shouts and energy for running. Jessie came outside without Mother.

"Jessie, help me turn the rope," Emily invited.

Allister and Jim had brought their bat and ball to school. Designating two sticks as home plate and first base, the twins soon had all the boys and a few of the girls practicing softball. When it was Sammy's turn, he brushed his curly, black hair out of his eyes, tensed his short, muscular body, swung the bat as if he was swatting at an attacking dog, and missed. Allister tried to give Sammy some tips, but the boy, with the flashing-brown eyes and dusky skin, just muttered a cuss phrase in French. Yanking the bottom of his long, loosely-fitting, tan shirt back under the woven, red sash around his waist, Sammy stomped away, causing his bare feet to raise small clouds of dust. *Going to school for the first time when you're thirteen*, Allister thought, *must be embarrassing as well as hard. I wonder where his family lives, and why he hasn't been to school before.*

After recess, it was time for arithmetic. Handing Jim a bunch of cards and two scribblers with an assignment in each, Miss French asked him to help Teena and John review their addition tables. Miss French gave Allister another set of cards to help Amy review her multiplication tables before she tried the assignment in her scribbler.

Once the other grades were busy, Miss French called up the first graders. Using several handfuls of small sticks, she helped them learn to count from zero to five and match the written number to the same number of sticks. Since many of the first graders had learned to write their numbers last year, she assigned a returning student to a new one to help them learn to write their numbers. The forty minutes for arithmetic seemed to pass in a flash.

At the end of arithmetic, Mother excused herself and Jessie. Allister overheard his mother explain to Miss French that they had to get home to make dinner for their family.

After a half hour of spelling for Grades 2 through 8 and letter writing review for the first graders, the teacher raised her hand as her silent cue for attention. "It's noon and time for our dinner break," she said. "Sammy, fill the wash basin that's sitting on the barrel stove with water from the pump. Everyone else, clear your desks. Then all of you who brought a dinner pail, line up to wash your hands before you eat. Those of you who walk home for dinner, you are dismissed."

As the twins climbed over a fence and crossed the pasture towards their barn, Allister asked, "Well, what do you think about our new teacher?"

"She's much too young," Jim said. "We're taller than she is, but ..."

"I think she's terrific!" Allister felt heat spread across his face. "If our father cooperates and doesn't pull us out of school as much as he did last year, we should have no trouble passing our exams and graduating from the eighth grade."

After dinner, Allister and Jim walked with Jessie back to school. Mother said she had a lot of work to do and that Jessie would be alright without her.

The first item on the afternoon's agenda was story time. When everyone had settled in their seat, Miss French sat where all could see the book she had in her hand.

"This morning we had a story about a chicken. This afternoon we're going to have a story about three little pigs and …. well, I won't spoil the surprise."

Allister leaned back in his desk, grinning from ear to ear. He knew the story, but he didn't really mind hearing it again. Now and again during the reading, Miss French paused to show the children the pictures in her book and ask her listeners a few questions. When she finished reading, she asked the first and second graders to draw a picture about the story. "If you want to, you can write a sentence or word under your picture."

While the lower grades were busy, Miss French called Amy, Jim, and Allister to her desk to start their first lesson in Canadian history. "Do you know from which country your family immigrated to Canada?" she asked. "Do you know when they did?"

"Our grandparents came from Scotland," Jim said.

"It was sixty or seventy years ago," Allister added, "but I don't know exactly when."

"Amy, do you know about yours?"

"No, Miss French. We've never talked about it."

"That's alright. Then that's your first homework assignment for history. Ask your parents, and then write a paragraph about your family history. The histories of your family and our nation are interesting stories. In the history scribbler I'm giving you, you'll find a reading assignment and a list of questions. Write the answers in full sentences, please."

———◆———

At the end of that first afternoon's recess, Miss French came out and, using her hand signal, silently stopped their play. "Please be seated on the grass there," she said, pointing. "Earlier today some of you drew a pig. When you did, what parts of the pig did you draw? Yes, John?"

"A head."

More hands went up. More parts of a pig were named.

"If you drew yourself, would you draw a tail?" the teacher asked. "Yes, Jimmy?"

"No, of course not. I don't have one!"

A ripple of chuckles travelled across the group of children.

"So," Miss French continued, "when a person draws a picture or a map of something, you draw a line around only what is there. Today, let's draw maps of each other. I'll pair you up—boys with boys and girls with girls. In the dirt, draw a line around your classmate while he or she lies flat on the ground. When you finish, raise your hand. I'll come and talk with you about the map you made of your schoolmate."

There was a lot of excited chatter as the students did their unusual task. When the teacher went around to the pairs, she asked for each to show where different parts of the body were in their maps: their classmate's neck, foot, hand. The upper grade students were asked about jaw, wrists, shins, palms, ankles, heel, thumbs, hips, knees, and throat.

Smiling to himself, Allister thought, *the younger students are learning about maps and all of us are learning body parts. I wonder when I'll get to learn about our bones and insides.*

Back in the schoolhouse, Miss French gave the upper grade students study time and paired the first graders to review their letters, letter words, and numbers. The second graders reviewed their reading assignment and their addition tables.

Fifteen minutes before the end of the school day, Miss French cued the stop of all activity. "Children, you have worked hard today. Everyone has done their very best. Now, it's time to put everything away."

Clutching his history and spelling homework, Allister looked over his shoulder as he exited the schoolhouse. The room looked exactly as it had when they entered it that morning. *At last,* he thought, as he breathed a sigh of relief, *we have an organized teacher. There's a place for everything, and everything's in its place.*

A short time later while he was walking with Jim and Jessie along the road from the schoolhouse to their farm lane, Allister saw Sammy ride a spotted, brown-on-white horse across their land towards Turtle Mountain.

———◆———

Mother continued to come to school with Jessie for a couple of hours every morning. Miss French seemed to accept the fact that it took Jessie four times longer than the other children to learn anything. Even with daily review of yesterday's schoolwork, Jessie's slow pace didn't seem to change.

Allister felt relief that the new school year seemed to have begun smoothly. *Eighth grade won't be so difficult, after all.*

chapter twenty

Smelly Feet

"**I** wouldn't do that if I were you." A boy's voice came from around of the corner of the schoolhouse during Thursday morning's recess.

"Ah, come on. It'll be fun. The big chicken won't do anything," another voice said.

"You better not," the first boy cautioned.

Overhearing the conversation between two schoolmates he couldn't see, Allister paused his rock toss game with his little sister, Jessie.

Apparently ignoring the first boy's advice, the second boy called loudly, "Hey, Alice Manure. Hey, stinky girl! Where's your apron? What do ya think you're doing, Alice?"

Allister groaned. When Will moved to his claim on the far side of their prairie, Allister had assumed that he wouldn't have to endure any more name-calling! *Now, here it is again*, he thought. *But who is doing it this time? No one at school did it last year!* He felt his temper flash red-hot. Doubling his fist, he took a step towards the taunting voice. Two small hands clasped his. Looking down, he saw Jessie hanging onto his fist.

"No, Allister. Mother say no fight," she said.

"Jessie, you're right." Allister leaned over to whisper into her ear. "Stand here. Say, 'What did you say?' real loud many times."

Jessie nodded.

With a glance over his shoulder at his sister, Allister trotted towards the back of the building.

He could hear Jessie holler, "What you say? What you say?"

That's right, Jessie. Keep his attention just a little longer.

"Hey, Alice Manure. Where's your apron? Aaa ... lice Ma ... nure! Where's your broom?"

While Jessie called to the taunter, Allister had made a loop behind the building and came up quickly behind the name-caller, who was saying, "You're such a g ..."

Whapping the other boy's knees with his own from behind, Allister sent the boy sprawling.

"Arggh!" The boy bit the dirt.

Grabbing an arm, Allister flipped his enemy onto his face. Sitting in the middle of his back, Allister yanked and twisted the flattened boy's arm behind his back.

The boy on the ground began to yell, "Get off me! Ow!"

Immediately a crowd gathered around the two.

Allister didn't move and kept twisting. "What's my name?" he demanded of the boy under him.

"Arggh!"

"No, that's not it! What's my name?"

"Aaaarggh! Let go! Sacre Bleu!"

"No cussing, in English or French! What's my name?"

The boy below him thrashed about, trying to kick Allister. Out of the corner of his eye, Allister saw someone grab the boy's buckskin leggings. When Allister turned to see who was helping him, he saw Jim pinning down the enemy's legs. Having done years of farm work, Allister was no featherweight, either.

"Mes côtes! You're breaking my ribs," the boy on the bottom complained.

"What's my name?" Allister repeated. "I'm not getting up until you say it correctly."

"Monsieur McRuer. Mr. Allister McRuer."

Standing up, Allister said, "You can let him up now, Jim."

Offering his hand, Allister pulled Sammy to his feet. "What's my name, Mr. Samuel Le Feete?" Allister said, looking stern.

"Mr. Allister McRuer," Sammy repeated.

"That's good, because if you'd called me anything else, I had a name for you."

"What was that?"

"Smelly Feet!"

Sammy let out a loud guffaw. "I guess we're even," he said.

"Yes, we are."

———◆———

When Jim and Allister left the schoolhouse that afternoon, Sammy was sitting astride his horse near the door. "Allister, want to come over to my house this afternoon?"

"Sorry, Sammy, got chores to do. Plus I'd need Mother's permission. Maybe tomorrow. Alright?"

"Mais oui!"

———◆———

That evening the conversation around the supper table turned tense when Father talked about taking time off from school for threshing again.

"Father, this time you really should talk to Miss French yourself," Allister said, steeling his nerves to voice his opinion. "Last year you had us tell our teacher that we'd be gone for two weeks. If either you or mother had gone to the teacher and requested permission for our absence, things would've gone a whole lot better."

When his suggestion was met with glum silence from his father, Allister pressed his point home by bringing up a second issue. "Besides, there's more at stake this year. Jim and I have eighth grade exams to pass in order to graduate. Any school we miss this year will make it that much harder for us. Neither Jim nor I are willing to ask for such a lengthy absence. You do it! Come on, Jim. Let's go put the livestock in for the night."

Jim hesitated, but then followed his twin out the back door. When they were out of earshot of the house, he said, "Golly, Allister, what made you take Father on like that?"

"Because last year he had us telling Mr. Webster, not asking. Remember? Well, you and I can't afford to miss two weeks this year. If Father has to talk to Miss French himself, I'll bet you my share of Mother's next pie that we won't have to miss any more than one week, because she'll make Father back down."

"You finagler, you." Jim grinned. "If it were up to just me, I'd rather spend two weeks in the fields than in a classroom any day."

"I know. Hang on, brother o'mine, it's only one more year. I need you ... no, I want you to finish with me, alright?"

"What about tomorrow?"

"Tomorrow?"

"Sammy's invitation?"

"Oh, I almost forgot. Jim, if you'll do my share of the chores with Jessie tomorrow, then I'll do yours and mine on Saturday. Deal?"

"Umm ... alright. Sammy didn't exactly invite me along."

"No, he probably has no idea that twins do everything together."

———————

On Friday afternoon, Allister shoved his lumpy book bag onto his back before he slid from the paddock's top railing onto the horse to ride behind Sammy. As their mount trotted towards the trail that led up Turtle Mountain, Allister saw Jim climb over their pasture fence, carrying both stacks of their homework assignments. At the same time, Father left their lane to head for the school.

Right now, Allister didn't want to think about his father's conference with Miss French. This was his first chance to visit the home of a friend his own age. He couldn't be happier. "Sammy, where does your family live?"

"Near a lake. At the end of this trail."

"Oh, we call it Lake William."

"The Lakota probably have another name for it, but I don't know what it is. My mother, Stalking Deer, speaks Cree, not Lakota."

"And your father speaks French."

"How did you know that?"

"Your name. Your cussing."

Sammy chuckled. "Allister, you speak some French, don't you?"

"Oui. Un peu."

"How did you learn? Neither of your parents speak French, do they?"

"No, they don't. I learned to speak French because my family used to live in Quebec. Jim and I went to a school that had a lot of French-speaking students. We learned from our schoolmates and neighbours."

The trail wound past boulders and trees to a clearing around the lake. On the far side of the area, Allister saw a roomy tepee and a tiny cabin.

"Our summer and winter lodgings," Sammy said, pointing at the tepee and then the cabin. "My mother is the only one at home right now. My father is working with a logging crew on the other end of the mountain."

Allister slid to the ground. Sammy removed the mare's bridle and turned her loose to graze near the lake. "Blue Eye actually belongs to my mother," Sammy said, "but she lets me ride her because the school is a long walk from here."

"Blue Eye! Why does Stalking Deer call her Blue Eye?"

"Because she's an unusual horse. She has one blue eye."

"She does? How did I miss that?"

A mahogany-skinned woman with two long, thick, black braids came out as Allister and Sammy approached the tepee. Allister was surprised to see that the woman was wearing a ruffled, maroon, cotton blouse above a fringed buckskin skirt, a blend of clothing from two cultures. But her jewelry was definitely Cree—a necklace and a pair of earrings made from mussel shells and held in place by leather thongs. A broad smile creased her handsome face when she looked at her son. After scrutinizing Allister with her deep brown eyes, she seemed to register amusement at his appearance. "Sky eyes like horse. Fire hair on poplar tree."

Although Allister was surprised by Stalking Deer's description of him, he had to smile at its frankness and perception. *So Sammy's mother speaks some English.*

"Allister, this is my mother, Stalking Deer."

Sammy's mother put out her hand and held it there until Allister reached out and shook it. "Come," she said, gesturing with her open palm.

Inside the cone-shaped, skin tent, Allister looked around. A few skin bags hung from the tepee's poles. Other skins with their fur side up covered the earthen floor. A fire inside a ring of rocks crackled and wisps of white-gray smoke lazily rose through the opening at the top of the tent. Because its sides were rolled up several inches, the tepee was airy, cool, and surprisingly smoke-free.

With Sammy acting as interpreter at times for her Cree, Stalking Deer asked Allister a number of questions. "She wants to know where your grandfather came from."

"Scotland."

"She says that her grandfather came from that same country. What was your grandfather's name?"

"McRuer."

"Hers was Sutherland. She says her grandfather and father were trappers and fur traders. What was your grandfather?"

"A farmer."

"Where was your father born?"

"Quebec."

"She wants to know if Quebec is part of Canada. I told her it is east, but it isn't across the big salt water. Maybe if you told her how many days it took you to get to Turtle Mountain from there, that would help."

"My family came by train in two boxcars. It took two weeks."

"Train? She doesn't know about a train."

"Tell her it's an iron horse with smoke and a loud whistle that rides on an iron trail from the east. She's probably seen one near Cherry Creek or Desford."

There was a moment of wide-eyed laughter and excited chatter in Cree. "She just told me a story about how scared she was the first time she saw one near Deloraine. So your family came on one of those from the east?"

"Yes, with our animals, farm equipment, and things for our house, like furniture, kitchen supplies, clothes, and such."

"She says, 'too many things.' We can put everything we own on the tepee poles for Blue Eye to pull. How many children does your mother have?"

"Seven."

"Is Jessie your only sister?"

"No, I have one other. She's married and lives with her husband on a farm several miles away."

"Is Jim older or younger than you?"

"Neither."

"Neither?"

"We're twins. Have the same birthday. Sammy, is Stalking Deer alright? She looks excited."

Sammy talked with his mother a few minutes in Cree. "She told me a story from the elders of the Hidastu, another tribe to the south. English people call this kind of story a legend. According to this story, the spirit who populated the earth from the heavens had a sister. She gave birth to twins. At that time, there were monsters that roamed the earth and tried to harm the people. Her twin boys were given powerful arrows to defeat the monsters, so my mother believes that you and your twin brother will be given special tools to fight evil."

I've always known my twin to be one special brother, Allister thought. *But I've never had the idea that being a twin gave me any special significance.* "Please tell your mother that was a very interesting legend," he said. "Thank you for telling me."

The whole time they were talking, Stalking Deer was preparing their meal over the fire. She broke off two chunks from the round loaf of bannock she had baked and put them in a clay bowl along with two spoons made from an animal's horn. Handing the bowl to Sammy, she left the tepee.

After Sammy served the stew, Allister copied his friend in dipping both his spoon and pieces of his bannock in the savoury meat. He could taste turkey, cranberries, and some kind of tuber or root. When their clay bowl was empty, Sammy served more stew and bannock from the pot on the fire. "My mother will be delighted that you like her cooking, and she would want me to make sure my guest has enough to eat. But please go easy, Allister, if you're satisfied. You and I eat all of this? She'll go hungry."

"Thanks for telling me. In my family, men and women eat together."

Sammy dipped two tin cups of broth from another pot to finish their meal. After they'd sipped all their hot drink, Sammy suggested they leave so his mother could eat.

Picking up his lumpy book bag reminded Allister of the things his mother had given him. "Oh, I almost forgot. Before we go, could you call your mother back in? My mother wants me to give Stalking Deer a couple of gifts."

"Alright. I'll call her."

Allister wiped his hands on his pants and took the gifts out of his school bag. Handing them to Stalking Deer, he explained, "One is a scarf my mother knit, made from wool. In winter, you can wrap it around your neck to keep it warm. The other is a small packet of salt. My mother uses a little of it to flavour meat dishes."

Sammy leaned over and softly repeated in Cree what Allister had said.

"Let's go," Sammy said in English.

As they left the tepee, Allister thought he saw a tear slip down Stalking Deer's face, but he wasn't sure.

Out in the clearing, Allister could only see dark shapes. The sun had already dipped below the rocks called Turtle's Back that stood above Lake William. "I'd better head home," he said.

"I'll give you a ride."

Blue Eye came in a gallop at Sammy's whistle. Riding the horse bareback with only a bridle, Sammy clung to her mane and gripped her barrel with his legs as she wound her way down the steep slope in the semidarkness. Sitting directly behind Sammy, Allister hung onto his friend's sash. "Sammy, you know about my family. What about yours? Do you have any brothers or sisters?"

"Yeah, twelve … seven brothers and five sisters. But they're all older, married, some with children. They live a long way north."

"There's something else I'd like to know," Allister said. "Why haven't you ever been to school before?"

"We move a lot, probably because of my father's work. Neither of my parents can read or write. My mother says it'd be good if I could. My father thinks it's a waste of time. He thinks I should be out working. He was by the time he was eleven, even younger than I am. As things sit, my mother has talked him into letting me go to school, since this is the closest we've ever lived to one."

"Well, let's hope you can stay most of the school year. If you don't see either Jim or me next week, it'll be because our father has pulled us out of school to help with the harvest."

"Are you coming back?"

"Oh, yes, my mother wants her boys in school too!"

chapter twenty-one

Little Girl Lost

When Allister entered through the back door of their farm-house, his parents were sitting at the kitchen table, drinking cups of tea and talking. Allister helped himself to a cup and sat down next to his mother.

"Did you have any supper?" she asked.

"Yes, thank you, Mother. Although Sammy's mother didn't say anything, I'm sure she appreciated your gifts."

"What did she fix you boys for supper?"

"Turkey stew with bannock. It was good."

"Bannock ... someday I'd like to get the recipe for that."

"Did you meet Sammy's father, son?" Father asked.

"No, I didn't. Sammy told me he's working with a logging crew right now."

"Then chances are we'll run into him later," Father said. "Allister, I talked to your teacher today. Miss French says you're her best student. She didn't want me to pull you out of school at all. We finally reached a compromise—one week absence for harvest plus an hour after school for a couple of weeks to help you and Jim catch up."

As the twins climbed into bed that night, Allister said, "When we get back to school, let's thank Miss French for sticking up for us."

"You do it," Jim objected. "I'm not exactly excited about staying after."

"Alright, Mr. Grumpy, but it's for our own good!"

———

The noisy gang of men and machines arrived early the first Tuesday of September. As the teams, wagons, thresher, and steam engine filled the farmyard, Mother came out of the house to count noses. "Oh boy, feeding twenty extra men for two days will certainly be a big job," Allister overheard his mother say to Caroline. "What are we going to do without Mary? At the very least, she provided a second pair of eyes on Jessie."

Caroline smiled. "Don't worry, we'll manage. I'm sure Mary's got her hands full at her and Joe's place these days."

Because no one had the time to take Jessie back and forth, she had been pulled out of school too. Mother said that she was afraid Jessie would get lost if she tried the half mile walk by herself.

Allister had no time to offer to monitor Jessie. He, Jim, and Dan were making repeated trips to the pump house, hauling extra drinking water for the men, and water for the teams and the steam engine. Taking turns driving their team of Clydesdales or pitching the bundles of wheat and feeding the hungry thresher ate up the rest of the morning.

This was Allister's third harvest on the Manitoba prairie. He was taller and his daily workout with the "pitchfork brigade" had made him stronger. Much to his relief, there was no Will to taunt or tease him this year. Although at thirteen Allister still wasn't able to keep up with John and Dan, things were easier for him than last year.

During the dinner break, Allister and Jim helped Mother and Caroline serve the threshing crew from behind the plank and sawhorse tables that had been made for Mary's wedding. "Hey, Jim, remember last year?" Allister said as they carried additional platters of food to the "tables."

"Yep. Don't have to use doors from the house as tables this year," Jim grinned. "'Got to give Mother credit, though. She's resourceful."

Intending to help carry out something else, Allister re-entered the kitchen just in time to see his little sister reach for the enamel coffee pot. "No, Jessie! Better let me bring that!" Allister grabbed her hand to stop her.

Jessie's face fell and her lower lip stuck out in a pout. She looked as if she were about to cry.

"Here, you can help the most by taking this basket of hard-boiled eggs to mother, alright?"

Jessie's face changed into a smile. "Eggs for Mother?"

Allister nodded. "That's right."

Appearing content at being able to help after all, Jessie shuffled out the door, basket in hand. Allister breathed a sigh of relief. Disaster averted. *One more moment, she'd have scalded herself with that hot pot. Wish Mary were here to keep an eye on her.*

At sunset after a picnic supper, some of the crew got back in their wagons and headed home. The supervisor and the rest set up tents or lay blankets under their wagons and settled in for the night. Father, John, and Dan turned the extra teams of horses into the south pasture. Jim, Allister, and Jessie did the chores for their own cattle and chickens.

Before he entered the house, Allister dusted himself off, dunked his head in the trough, and shook off the water like a dog shaking after a dip. Taking a bath was pointless. Tomorrow was going to be another day full of grain dust.

At daybreak, Allister and Jim were up to help Mother and Jessie make breakfast for the crew and family while Father, John, and Dan did most of the chores. When they were almost ready to eat, Mother asked Jim to set up a washstand, and Allister to bang on a pot outside next to the back door. When John came, Mother posted him at the door to make sure everybody washed up. For the next forty-five minutes, Jim, Allister, and Jessie were kept busy making sure everyone had all the oatmeal, scrambled eggs, pancakes, Angus beef steak, sliced bread, blueberry pie, and drink they wanted. When the threshing fellas finished, Mother had Caroline join her in the kitchen to have a cup of coffee while the children ate breakfast. "Jim, Allister, when you're done, go out to the fields. We ladies will clean up in here. Father says they'll probably finish this afternoon."

True to Father's forecast, the crew finished threshing and bagging the last bundle of wheat about an hour after their noon dinner break. Everyone helped move the threshing unit to Thomas' farm. With the clatter of machinery, the rumble of wagons, and the clop of horse hooves disappearing into the distance, the usual quiet of the farmyard returned.

Allister and Jim were putting the plank table tops away when they heard a scream. Running around the corner of the machinery shed, the boys heard it again, coming from the house. Just as they reached the back door, Mother came running out. "Jessie!" she cried.

Seeing Allister and Jim, she asked, "Have either of you seen Jessie? I've checked the house from top to bottom. She's not there."

"The outhouse?" Jim suggested.

"The chicken coop?" Allister asked.

"The barn?" Mother fled in that direction.

Minutes later, the three met in the middle of the farmyard. Running in different directions, they checked other places. "Jessie! Jessie! Jessie!" echoed around the homestead. Jim and Allister scrambled into every corner of the barn loft, around every straw stack and grain bin, and behind every cow.

"Go get Father, Jim," Mother said, handing him Shalazar's bridle. "Allister, help me get him. He can be a handful."

Jim's apprehension proved correct. Rearing and backing, the horse complicated Allister's and Jim's efforts to get the bridle on him.

"I think Shalazar is sensing our panic," Jim sputtered during the struggle, "and he's panicking too."

After the twins had succeeded in getting the bridle on the nervous horse, and Allister had a firm enough grip on the reins close to the bit, Jim vaulted onto Shalazar's back. "Alright, Allister. Let go!"

Allister did, and Jim dug his heels into the horse's flanks. Shalazar made flying leaps down the lane and around the corner onto the road heading west. In a breath, all Allister could see of horse and rider was a cloud of dust.

A sob behind him made Allister turn around. There was his mother in a crumpled heap in the dirt. Dropping to the ground next to her, he put his arms around his obviously distraught mother. *She's been so brave through so much already. I, too, am scared to death what might happen to Jessie.* Blinking furiously, Allister fought to control his own flood of tears that threatened. *Got to stay calm. Keep a clear head.*

"I'm sorry," she said, wiping away her tears. "Ever since we came west, I've feared this very thing—losing Jessie. And now it's come true. Yesterday and today I was so busy, I didn't have time to keep track of her every minute. Until Mary got married, I always had a second pair of eyes on our little girl. Now I don't. That's been so hard."

"Jessie can't walk long distances. Doubt she's gone far, Mother. Where was the last place you saw her?"

Mother got up and walked over to the picnic dinner area. "I was here and she was there," she said, pointing.

Allister walked to the spot his mother had indicated and studied the ground. He could see where his sister had sat in the grass and rolled over to stand up. Drag marks in the dirt and through the grass showed the direction Jessie had limped—away from the fields and farmyard towards Turtle Mountain. *Why has Jessie gone anywhere? I've never known her to be adventurous. She usually sticks pretty close to Mother when there are strangers about.* He stood, studying the grass ahead of him for movement.

The stillness around him was broken by the sound of many men and horses. News about Jessie's disappearance had spread. All the neighbours and threshing crew came to help. Those with big draft horses they could ride sat on them, looking and calling.

"John, give a sharp whistle, would you? Let's organize this search. We've got a lot of tall grass to beat our way through," Father said from the middle of the farmyard.

When all the volunteers had gathered, Father had them form a line with no more than three feet between each person to do the sweeps. Based on what Allister had found, they started from the picnic area and moved towards Turtle Mountain, calling for Jessie as they went. Hours passed. Supper time came and went. The search continued without interruption.

The sun set. Father and John returned to the barn to get several lanterns. An hour after darkness fell, the searchers straggled back.

When Allister finally gave up the search in the dark, he found Mother standing by the back door with a lit kerosene lamp in her hand. "Everyone has gone home. They told me they'd begin again at first light. It's too dry for everyone to be walking about with lit lanterns or lamps. The last thing we need is a huge grass fire."

His mother's comment gave Allister a frightening picture. *No, Lord God, don't let that happen. Jessie is in plenty of danger without a prairie on fire, too.* Fear practically stole his breath away. *Calm yourself, Allister. Think about what you should do now.*

"Reverend Wood told me to ask God for help whenever I need it. Let's do that now."

Mother nodded. Together they bowed their heads.

"God, Jessie is lost," Allister prayed. "We don't know where she is, but You do. Keep her safe and send someone to bring her back to us. In Your Son Jesus' name. Amen."

When Allister looked up, Mother's tearful face appeared relaxed for the first time that day. "She's in the safest hands, son," Mother said. "Thanks for that reminder."

Before he climbed into bed that night, Allister asked for one more thing. "God, please keep Jessie safe from the wolves and give her a warm place to sleep."

———◆———

At daybreak, Allister joined his father and brothers as they hurried through their usual routine of chores. Mother baked piles of biscuits and made several pots of tea to share with the searchers when they arrived. Father and John organized the threshing crew and neighbours in a line to sweep through a different section between the barnyard and Turtle Mountain.

In case Jessie came back on her own, Mother kept close to the house and asked Allister to stay nearby to act as a runner, if needed.

While they were waiting, she gave him the task of digging up the potatoes in the garden.

While he worked, he fretted. *How can anyone find one small girl in those many acres of tall grass? There are miles of it between here and Turtle Mountain. Surely, she couldn't have walked as far as the mountain. If she has, how can she stay safe up there?* The worrisome questions cycled around and around in his mind. Trying to calm himself, he prayed for the searchers.

Midmorning, Allister heard Mother calling him. As he approached their farmyard at a run, he saw Stalking Deer standing in front of Mother, holding a child by the hand. Just then, the Cree woman let go, and Jessie stumbled into Mother's arms. While Mother and Allister watched, Stalking Deer told her story through pantomime and a few French or English words.

"She says," Allister told his mother, "when the sun came up she left her tepee to gather wood. When she came back, she went into the cabin next to the tepee. While she was stacking the wood inside, she saw Jessie in the cabin's bed. When Jessie woke up, Stalking Deer gave Jessie some bannock and water. Jessie asked for her family. She said, 'Allister,' so Stalking Deer brought her here. At times, she carried Jessie because of her bad leg. Merci beaucoup," Allister said, reaching for the Cree woman's hand.

With tears running down her face, Mother thanked Jessie's rescuer. Allister and Mother smothered Jessie in hugs. When they looked up again, Stalking Deer was gone.

Allister knelt in front of his sister. "Jessie, why did you leave?"

"Pretty kitty. Black and white. I see kitty. I say 'Come here.' She run away. I try to catch. I call. She run some more. Soon no kitty. I look and look. Then our house get lost. I climb up rocks. I look. No house. I see trail. I walk and walk. I sit. I walk. I see small house. No family. I'm cold. It dark. In house, bed. I go to bed."

Allister looked up at Mother. "A black and white kitty?" he repeated, puzzled.

"A skunk!" they said together.

"Jessie followed a skunk," Mother said. "Evidently it didn't spray her. She's lucky."

"We're all lucky!" Allister said. "And God answered all our prayers for Jessie!"

"That He did!" Mother smiled. "We need to thank Stalking Deer for her part in Jessie's rescue. When you return to school next week, I'll give you a gift to pass on to Sammy for her.

"Now you'd better run; call off the search. Our little lost girl is home, safe and sound."

Relieved that Jessie had been found, the neighbours and threshing crew returned to their harvesting. Allister and Jim worked alongside the crew at Thomas' and Joe's. By the end of the week, the twins had also helped Mother finish most of the harvesting of the garden. John and Dan continued with the threshing crew for several weeks and later worked at Morton's sawmill on Turtle Mountain to get lumber for Dan's claim.

Father stayed home. There was grain to haul to the elevators. He had to sell some as feed, since the early frost had damaged it too much for it to be ground into flour. Field and garden had to be plowed before the winter's snow buried everything.

Miss French kept her promise to spend extra time helping the twins catch up on their studies. Allister thoroughly enjoyed digging into his assignments. He continued to help Sammy. Between Miss French's instruction and Allister's one-on-one tutoring, the boy from Lake William learned to sound out words as he learned to read.

Some afternoons after school, Sammy gave Jessie a ride home on Blue Eye. Then he kept Allister and Jim company as they did their chores. Sometimes he helped. When Mother invited him to stay for supper, he always accepted with a pleased grin. "Scones and tea aren't bannock and broth, but they taste good too," he'd always say.

A blizzard unexpectedly smothered the area around Wood Lake School a week before the Christmas Pageant was supposed to close the fall term. The pageant was cancelled and school was closed a week early for Christmas vacation and the lengthy winter break. There were a lot of unhappy Wood Lake School students. But none of them could have guessed how dangerous to children this winter would prove to be.

chapter twenty-two

Trusting a Horse?

Two weeks of mild weather had finally come. It was April of 1895. The mountains of snow had mostly melted.

One Saturday, Father sent Allister to check and repair the fence around the south pasture. Harnessing Jake to the stone boat, fourteen-year-old Allister took a shovel, a saw, a hammer, staples, a roll of barb wire, and posts with him. While he worked on reattaching loose wires, he thought about Sammy and Stalking Deer. In February, when school reopened, Sammy hadn't returned. Several Saturdays later, Allister talked Jim into walking up to Lake William with him. There they found the cabin, deserted, the tepee no longer beside it. Sammy and his family were gone. Allister felt disappointment for his friend. Too bad. Sammy had been so excited about learning to read.

Totally absorbed in his thoughts, Allister paid no attention to the weather. Only when something cold and wet struck his face did he notice that the wind had shifted and a dark, flat-bottomed cloud covered the sky above the McRuer farm. *Plop. Plop-plop.* Gigantic, wet flakes fusing crystal with crystal rapidly coated grass, horse, stone boat, fence posts, and even the barb wire. The wind died and the temperature dropped. To Allister, it felt as if the area around him had turned into a down shaft of icy air. Within two breaths, heavy snow blanketed everything. The day that had started out mild was now miserably cold.

Allister glanced along the one section of the fence he had almost completed. *Should I stay and finish, or head back to the house?* The snow was falling so thickly around him he could no longer see the house. He could barely see the fence on the other side of the pasture.

"Alright, Jake, we've done enough for today." Turning the horse around, Allister led him along the fence to the gate. Staring into the white curtain directly in front of him, Allister hesitated. If he led Jake into the whiteout, they might wander in a circle and miss the barn or the house altogether.

He remembered a story that had spread around the Cherry Creek and Desford area that winter. A farmer with his little daughter on his back had done just that. The man had gone out to his barn to tend to his animals one evening. When he stumbled the next morning into another homesteader's house, he was miles away from where he had started, had been walking all night, and the child he carried on his back had frozen to death. Allister thought about the little girl's terrible end and trembled.

Within moments, his situation grew worse. He could no longer see anything on either side of him, neither the fence post nor the horse. Running one hand along the rein he was holding, Allister felt his way along the horse to the harness traces attached to the stone boat Jake was pulling. Unhitching him, Allister climbed onto the Clydesdale's broad back. Dropping the reins across Jake's withers, Allister nudged his mount with his heels. "Barn, boy. Find the barn." The horse lowered his head and plodded into the smothering wet, white wasteland.

Allister pulled his hat down over his ears as far as he could. With one hand, he held the top of his coat closed. He stuffed his other under Jake's harness collar, hoping the hand resting on the horse's shoulder would stay warm and the grip on the leather collar would keep Allister on Jake. *So sleepy. Don't want to fall off.* This surprise of a spring storm had caught Allister without a sweater, a scarf, or a pair of mittens. *And to think I'd almost come out without a hat or coat!*

Jake marched steadily on. The pelting snow caked the horse. Allister felt the cold, white flakes blanket him as well. He closed his eyes to protect them from the ice crystals forming on his eyelashes. Within minutes, they were frozen shut. *Oh no. Can't see at all.* Switching hands, he tried to rub the ice away. He tried again and again, giving the hand under the horse's collar time to warm up before using it again to wipe. *Still can't see anything.*

Losing all sense of time, Allister muttered, "Is it morning yet? Did I finish the fence? Where am I? Oh no, I didn't finish the chores. Father will be angry. Why am I riding a horse? How long have I been on him?" *I am so cold. All I want to do is sleep.*

"Allister, stay awake!" he scolded out loud. But he couldn't keep his head from nodding. While his mount moved on, Allister dozed.

Jake suddenly stopped and Allister fell off. Warm, moist breath and the horse's soft muzzle brushed Allister's cheek. He tried to open his eyes. *Aargh! I still can't see anything.* He put out his hand. Rough wood. The barn! Allister laughed. "Good boy, Jake. You saved our lives."

Allister scrambled to his feet and felt his way along the building until he found the barn door. Once inside, he collapsed onto a mound of hay and waited for the crystals on his eyelashes to thaw. When he could finally see, Allister smiled at the velvety nostrils breathing warm air onto him, and the snow-covered head and ears of the horse standing over him. Gratefully wiping the melting snow off himself and Jake, Allister unharnessed and rewarded his rescuer with hay and grain.

My next challenge is to make it to the back door of the house I can't even see. Allister shuddered at the thought of leaving the warmth of the barn and enduring more of the cold. *If I don't get home soon, Mother will be worried to death.* Remembering what his brothers had done to find him and Jim during a whiteout last year, he tied lengths of rope together until he thought they could reach across the distance between the barn and the house. Tying one end to the metal ring next to the barn door and the other around his waist, he walked into the storm until he reached the end of his lifeline. Shuffling right, he stumbled onto the wood pile. Shuffling left, he bumped into the corner of the house. When he untied the rope around his waist, it was just long enough to tie it to the hook next to the back door. Barely able to see and stumbling inside, Allister felt arms around his waist and another pair around his shoulders. Other hands brushed him off.

"We thought you got lost." Jessie clung to Allister, hugging him again and again.

"Glad you're home alright." Mother sighed and put her warm hands on his frost-bitten face. "We were so worried. The weather turned so suddenly, there was no time to send someone out to bring you back."

"This whiteout was worse than the one when you and Jim spent the day in the barn," Father said. "That time you had shelter, but this time, you were out in the open. How did you get back, son?"

"Mounted Jake and gave him his head. He brought us to the barn," Allister said. "He's in the barn now, warm and fed. I used your rope trick, John, to find the house. It's tied between the house and barn now."

"Guess there's some truth to 'horse sense,'" Jim joked.

"Maybe knowing which horse to trust is closer to the point," Allister countered.

———◆———

That night before he dropped off to sleep, Allister whispered a prayer: "It wasn't really the horse, was it? It was You, wasn't it, God? Thank you for guiding Jake to the barn. Thank you for looking out for Jake and me."

chapter twenty-three

Warnings Ignored

"Allister! Jim!" John called from the back door one Saturday morning. "A couple of Clydesdales are for sale. Dan and I are going to take a look. Want to come along?"

Glancing at Jim who was also hunched over his books on the dining room table, Allister rolled his eyes and muttered, "Oh brother. Don't they know we have mounds of studying to do for the upcoming eighth grade exams?" Shaking his head, he thought, *Spring's here. John and Dan are like a team of horses, chomping on the bit to get going. Without enough draft horses to work all three claims, I guess they will have to do something to get more horses. But why involve us? We have our own work to do.*

Ignoring what Allister said, Jim jumped up and ran towards the back door. Allister hollered after him, "Jim, we've got to stick to our studies!" Allister might as well have saved his breath. Jim went. Allister stayed. This scenario repeated itself many times during the next couple of months.

True to his word, Dan never asked either brother to skip school to help him work on his claim. The only time he accepted Jim's help was after school and on weekends. But every hour that Jim could've studied, he helped his older brothers farm. Any time Allister asked his twin when he planned to study for his exams, Jim's answer was always, "Later."

Victoria Day holiday weekend came. All of the family worked on Mother's garden and resettled the chickens in their chicken coop's new location ... all of the family except Allister. After he'd finished his regular chores, he bent over his books. *I've only got a couple of weeks 'til those exams at the end of June*, Allister fretted.

In early June, Father and the three brothers harrowed the fields with the two teams of Clydesdales on all three claims—Father's, John's, and Dan's. Allister studied.

When the opportune week for planting came, Father insisted that both Allister and Jim set aside their books for seed broadcasters. Every day after school and on weekends, including Sundays, the twins were pressed into planting. The broadcasting continued until Father's one hundred acres of wheat and twenty acres of oats, John's thirty acres of wheat, and Dan's twenty acres of wheat and ten acres of oats, were plant-ed. After each long day of school and planting, Allister studied until his mother insisted he get to bed.

The very last weekend of June, Jim brought all his books and scrib-blers home. Laying them out on the dining room table, he said, "Alright, Allister, what do I study?"

"You mean stuff into your brain, don't you?"

"Well, I have two days. What do you suggest?"

Allister felt like punching his brother and saying, "You idiot! Why haven't you studied before this?" But he didn't.

Going through each subject, he made a list of information to study and numbers of pages to read. "I'll quiz you Sunday evening if you'd like me to," Allister offered.

Settling behind his own pile of books and notes, he reviewed ev-erything that Saturday morning. Feeling confident as he stretched the stiffness out of his limbs from sitting so long, Allister thought, *Well, I've studied anything that might possibly be on those exams. Guess I'm as ready as any-body could get.* After dinner at noon, Allister finished the detailed map of Canada that was due by the end of the term. *There! I've completed all my school projects, too. I know Jim hasn't even started his. Too bad. That map will probably be on the exam.*

After supper, Jim returned to the dining room to study. Allister did both his chores and Jim's. When he came back in the house, Jim was sit-ting in the dark. Allister lit the kerosene lamp on the table and said, "A little light on the subject might help."

"Thanks."

Deciding not to wait for his brother, Allister took a bath and went to bed. Sometime during the night, he felt Jim climb in.

When Allister woke up Sunday morning, he realized Jim hadn't bothered to undress. Letting his twin get a few more winks, Allister went out to the barn and did both their chores again. As Allister left the house for church, Jim was sitting at the dining room table, studying.

Leaving his twin hard at work after the noon meal, Allister decided he could take time for a walk with his mother and little sister up the trail to Lake William. They took turns pulling Jessie in a little wagon Dan had built for her. Along the way, Jessie asked Allister to pick dandelions because "they are yellow like the sun." When she saw the cabin by the lake, she got excited. "I follow kitty here. I sleep in this house."

"That wasn't a kitty." Allister frowned and shook his head. "That was a skunk! Skunks can give you a big, bad stink. Jessie, when you see a furry, black animal with a white stripe down its back, you run away from it. Do not try to catch it!"

"That's right, Jessie," Mother said. "Stay away from the skunk!"

"Alright, no sunk."

After a brief look inside the cabin and a walk around part of the lake, Mother led the way home.

That evening, Allister once again did both his and Jim's chores. Turning on the kerosene lamp for his brother, Allister kept his promise. For two hours he quizzed Jim on spelling, grammar, reading vocabulary, Canadian history and geography, and arithmetic. The last subject was the only one Jim seemed to know really well.

"Hmm. Guess you need to study some more," Allister said when it was their usual bedtime. Leaving Jim to pour over his history book, Allister went upstairs to bed. An hour later, Jim climbed in with his clothes on—again.

Monday morning was exam day. Jim was up early and already studying when Allister came downstairs. Without a word, he did double chores again and ate breakfast. At 8:40, he put his homework into his book bag. "Come on, Jim. It's time!"

Grabbing a slice of bread as he headed out the door, Jim ran after Allister across the pasture and vaulted the fence.

The silence of the usually noisy schoolyard seemed eerie. Since it was exam day for the eighth graders, none of the other students came. Entering the building, the boys found Miss French and the district superintendent waiting for them. Allister gave the teacher his map of Canada, pages of penmanship, and his scribblers with arithmetic, reading, vocabulary, and history assignments for her to mark.

Seating Jim and Allister on opposite ends of the room, the superintendent, who was to proctor their exam, gave them their test papers and blank scribblers. "No talking," he said. "You must not help each other. If you have a question, you must raise your hand. When I come to you, ask me your question. The best way to take an exam is to read through the whole test first to see which part will take you the most time. Do the other parts quickly so that you have the most time for the hardest one. Write your answers in the scribblers, not on the test paper. You have one hour for this section."

Allister followed the instructions, looking through the whole test before he started to answer anything. The last part of the test would take the longest time to do, so he hurried through the first three parts of this combination exam of grammar, spelling, vocabulary, and reading comprehension. The next time he turned to look at the clock on the back wall, he had ten minutes left. He'd finished the test. There was time to check some of his work. Before the time was up, he handed his papers to the proctor. Jim was still scribbling as fast as he could when the man asked for the papers.

The second test was arithmetic. Allister figured he'd have more trouble with this than Jim. An hour and fifteen minutes later, however, they'd both finished this section, early.

"It's noon and time for your dinner break," the proctor said. "Your teacher told me that you eat dinner at home. Leave your book bags and everything else here. We'll see you at one o'clock."

Allister and Jim stopped at the school pump for a drink. They ambled across the schoolyard, climbed up on their father's pasture fence, and sat a moment—to allow their brains to rest.

"Well, Jim, how are you doing?" Allister finally asked. "These last three days have been like a Greek Olympic marathon for you with your nonstop studying, little sleep, and no breakfast, to speak of, this morning."

"You know those refried potatoes that Mother fixes from leftovers?"

"Uh-huh. Toasted on the outside, mushy on the inside?"

"Yeah. That's what my brain feels like right now."

"On which test do you think you did better?"

"The arithmetic."

"Let's go ask Mother for some brain food."

The afternoon's exams weren't any easier. There was an hour and a half of history. By the time Allister finished that one, names and dates were spinning like the wheels on his mother's buggy. This was followed by an hour for geography. Part of the test was a blank outline map on which he had to draw and label Canada's mountains, rivers, lakes, provinces, capitals, islands, and oceans. He was very glad he had already completed his map project.

When they had sweated through the last of it, Jim didn't say a thing all the way home or through their evening chores. That night, Allister was awakened several times by Jim's twisting and turning.

Before ringing the school bell to start the school day the next morning, a glum-faced Miss French called in the twins one at a time, Jim first. *This can't be good news*, Allister thought. When it was his turn to get his exam marks, he was surprised by the look on his teacher's face. *She must have been crying*, he thought. *Jim looked upset, but he didn't tell me what happened.*

When Miss French opened up his exam papers, Allister was overwhelmed with relief. He'd passed everything, and his history, geography, vocabulary, and reading marks were excellent. "Thank you, Miss French," Allister said. "When I came in here and saw your face, I was sure I'd flunked eighth grade."

"No, Allister. I'm upset, but not because of you. You've done an excellent job this year. It's your brother. His mind must have been elsewhere. I've given him a note to give your parents. I need to talk to them. I'm telling you because I want you to make sure he gives it to them. Alright?"

"Of course."

The next three and a half days of school were awkward for Allister. Since he'd already completed everything, he spent most of his time helping the teacher ... and Jim, when he could. It was hard to watch his twin struggle with the completion of work when his heart wasn't in it at all.

Mother and Father had come to talk to Miss French. An agreement had been reached. If Jim finished his homework assignments and completed his map project by Friday morning, Miss French would give him marks for the year and a certificate of eighth grade attendance at the Friday night's closing presentation. But he wouldn't graduate. The arithmetic section of his exams was the only part he had passed.

Mr. McRuer's reaction to Jim's situation surprised Allister. *No blow up. I expected him to be really angry, but Father simply shrugged, said he'd struggled in school too. On the other hand, Mother said just what I thought she would. I overheard her tell Jim she was disappointed he hadn't done well enough to graduate.*

The fun of the races and games on Field Day was over. All the students had polished the schoolhouse spotless for the final program. But the event that Allister had eagerly anticipated all year had lost its lustre. *I feel sorry for Jim. I so wanted him to graduate with me. He won't be sharing in my joy.*

That evening, parents, siblings, and neighbours packed the lantern-lit schoolhouse for Wood Lake School's second closing event. Samples of the students' work covered the bulletin board and much of the walls for all to see. Mother led the audience and the children in various songs with her pump organ. All of the children who could read recited a short piece from their reading texts, with one exception. Jim refused to participate.

As the only graduating eighth grader, Allister was the very last to recite. He stood alone on the platform and looked out over the crowd. Standing near the door was a farmer he recognized—his older brother, Will! Allister blinked in surprise. *He came after all. I didn't think he would!*

Gulping and looking at Mother and Jim to steady his nerves, he began the speech he had prepared. "During my eight years in school, I have read many stories. One of the world's best storytellers was Jesus. His stories are in the Bible, and they are called parables. Some of Jesus' parables are explanations about the kingdom of heaven. Here is one He told that is recorded in the book of Matthew, *"For the kingdom of heaven is as a man travelling into a far country, who called his own servants, and delivered unto them his goods. And unto one he gave five talents, to another two, and to another one, to every man according to his several ability; and straightway took his journey...*[6]

Allister recited the rest of the parable, telling what happened when the master of the servants returned to get an accounting of the goods given them.

"There is more to the story," Allister continued, "but I won't recite it here. You can read more about it in Matthew 25. Reverend Forsythe told me that the talents in this story were actually certain quantities of money, but I like to think of these talents in the parable as abilities. God has given each of us abilities, some less, some more. The important point isn't how much or how many. The important point is endeavouring to use, not bury, one's talents. It is my plan to use every talent God has given me and to develop more."

At the end of his speech, Allister bowed as the audience clapped. After he had squeezed onto the bench next to Jim, the teacher handed out awards. The first one was to Jessie for learning to write the whole alphabet in capital letters. First prizes for penmanship were given to Etta and Allister. Amy won an award for being the best speller at their weekly Friday afternoon spelling bees. Two best-in-geography certificates were given to Amy and Allister. And Jim won the award for best in arithmetic again.

After the school board members came to the front, Miss French said, "Jim and Allister McRuer, please come to the platform. Wood Lake School families, these were our eighth grade students this year."

Without comment, she handed Allister and Jim their certificates. The school board members and she shook hands with both boys, and the gathering was dismissed. Much to Allister's relief, nothing was said in public about Jim's exam failure. Yet when Allister compared his certificate with Jim's, his said he had graduated and Jim's said he had attended the eighth grade, just as Miss French had promised.

"Sorry, Jim. I really wanted us to graduate together," Allister said. "I'm disappointed. Aren't you?"

"It's my own fault. You tried to warn me, but I refused to listen. It doesn't really matter much. I wasn't planning on more schooling anyway."

Some loud thumping on their backs interrupted their conversation. Allister looked up to see the two of them surrounded by their three older brothers and Mary and Joe.

"This is great!" Allister exclaimed. "Thank you all for coming!"

As the crowd dispersed, Miss French gave Jim and Allister their marked papers, scribblers, and report cards. In return, the twins gave their teacher a small gift from their mother. "Miss French," Allister said, "thank you for all your hard work with us this year. Thank you especially for your patience with Jessie."

At the McRuer farmhouse, Mary and Joe stayed long enough to eat a piece of Mother's yellow cake, drink some tea, commiserate with Jim, and congratulate Allister. Will, on the other hand, was spending the weekend. His dairy farm employer had given him Friday evening through Monday morning off for their Dominion Day celebration.

When Allister and Jim went out in the late evening twilight to take care of Will's horses and do chores, they saw a large packing crate in their brother's wagon. Something in the wooden box was whining. "I wonder what's in that crate," Allister said.

"Sounds like a puppy!" Jim exclaimed.

"A puppy? Why would Will be hauling a dog with him on a visit home?"

chapter twenty-four

A Tawny Toonie

Allister and Jim held Jessie's hands to keep her from pulling off her blindfold. Although Will had instructed her to sit still, Jessie squirmed on the dining room chair that he'd put next to the kitchen table. "Be real quiet, Jessie," he said. "Your eighth birthday will be here soon, but this present can't wait, so I had to bring your surprise in my wagon today. Wait there a minute. I'll bring it in."

Will left the kitchen and returned with a bundle of wiggly, brown and white fuzz. Placing it on his little sister's lap, he said, "Alright, Allister, take off Jessie's blindfold."

The girl squealed at the sight of the puppy on her lap. Frightened, the sable and white fluff-ball tumbled off and pattered across the floor. Scooping up the puppy, Will placed the dog in Jessie's lap once more. "Talk quietly, Jessie. Don't scare your puppy, now," he said, squatting in front of his sister. "Be gentle. Stroke her head and back like this."

"What kind of dog is that?" Allister asked.

"Your grandfather would've called her a toonie," Father said. "Most people in Canada know these dogs as Shetland Sheepdogs, or Shelties."

"Where did you get her?"

"Remember your friend, Randy, and his black and white herd dog?" Will asked. "Well, this little toonie is one of her puppies. She's seven weeks old. Just old enough to be taken from her mother."

"Jessie, what are you going to name your puppy?" Jim asked, stroking the dog's ears.

"Umm ... Tawny," Jessie said. "Father said she is a tawny, so I call her Tawny."

How did Jessie get tawny out of the word toonie? Allister wondered. *I doubt my little sis knows the meaning of the word "tawny," but the name fits her puppy perfectly.*

Out of a pant pocket Will pulled a leather collar and a leash with a clip on the end of it. "I made these for your puppy, Jessie. Let's put these on her."

Will showed Jessie how to buckle the collar around Tawny's neck. He undid it and handed the collar to his little sister. "Now you try, Jessie."

Jessie struggled with the buckle. Fastening anything to such a wiggly puppy seemed too much. "Tawny, hold still."

"I'll hold her," Will offered. "Jessie, you buckle."

"Good," Jim smiled. "You did it, Jessie."

Jessie beamed at everyone.

"Now, let's take your puppy outside," Dan said. "Maybe she needs her outhouse."

"Outhouse? Tawny has an outhouse?" Jessie asked.

"Come see," Dan said. In the dim light of the departing day, he led the family to the grove of poplar and elm. "Between these trees is a good outhouse for a puppy."

Jessie stood patiently while the puppy sniffed the ground here and there. Finally, she squatted and did her business.

"Now pet her and tell her, 'Good dog!' Every couple of hours you need to bring her out here," Will said. "She'll need to use her outhouse several times a day, and maybe even at night."

"It's Jessie's bedtime," Mother said. "Let's put Tawny's crate in a corner of Jessie's room for now."

Will carried the wooden box and a burlap sack upstairs. He dumped a layer of wood chips from the sack into the crate and covered the layer with the sack. "Rachel gave me these cedar chips to put in the bottom of the box," Will said when he saw Allister watching him. "She says the smell keeps out bugs."

"Oh, like the lining of Mary's hope chest," Allister murmured.

After Jessie was in bed and Tawny in her box, Mother came in the bedroom with an old towel sewn up. "Here, Allister, put this in next to Tawny. It's a wheat-stuffed pillow that I heated in the oven. The warm, lumpy wheat will be her substitute sibling for a couple of nights until she's used to being without her cuddling brothers and sisters."

Everyone except Jessie returned to the kitchen and sat around for a time, listening to the story swapping. But it'd been an exhausting week for Jim. He was next to bed. One by one, the family dismissed themselves to "count the cows that passed the gate" until Will and John were the only ones still up. In his bedroom above the kitchen, Allister heard their voices below late into the night.

Barely an hour into the next morning, an enormous commotion erupted on the edge of the farmyard. Allister dropped his pitchfork and ran from the barn towards the ruckus. He heard Jessie yelling, "No, Tawny. Bad dog. Stop it!" The excited yipping of the puppy and the squawking of frightened chickens continued.

When Allister got close enough to see what was going on, he didn't know whether to laugh or groan. Tawny had gotten loose and was chasing the chickens. Wings, feathers, and scrawny legs scrambled in every direction. Into the mayhem, Jessie lumbered, trying to catch her puppy.

"Jessie," Allister called, "let me help you get Tawny. Stand still!"

Jessie stopped and turned around. "Allister, she saw the chickens. Ran from me. Will she hurt them?"

Allister raced after the puppy. Lunging at the streaking fluff ball, he landed face down in the dirt, but still managed to grab the dog by the long hair on the back of her neck. When Allister rolled over, he had his arms wrapped around her and the puppy lying on his chest. "Jessie, I got her!"

Spitting dirt, feathers, and dog hair out of his mouth, Allister scrambled to his feet. Handing Jessie the end of Tawny's leash, Allister set the puppy on the ground in front his little sister. "Hang onto her real tight. Tawny's probably never seen a chicken before," Allister laughed. "I don't think she was trying to hurt them. After all, herding is her natural instinct. Maybe she was just trying to get the chickens into the coop … not a place they want to go at this time of day. Now don't scold her,

Jessie," Allister added. "Call her and ask her to follow you away from the chickens and the coop. Then tell her, 'Good dog,' when she obeys you."

Allister stayed nearby until Jessie had successfully coaxed Tawny into following her back to the house. *When Jessie wished for a puppy, she had no idea how much trouble such a pet could be.*

With five brothers to give directions, Jessie and Tawny learned together how a Sheltie could fit into the household. One thing was very clear from the beginning—Tawny was Jessie's pet. Mother insisted that Jessie, not her brothers, feed, water, groom, lead, and "outhouse" train her puppy. Mother had taken the precaution of putting small sections of wattle fencing in the doorways to the sitting room. She also kept the door to her own bedroom closed, but that didn't prevent accidents.

"Oh no, Tawny's made a mess," Jessie would say, sometimes several times in a day. "Not again!" It took Jessie quite a while to figure out when to take Tawny to her outhouse.

As Allister watched Jessie struggle in caring for her pet, he thought, *Tawny will be good for Jessie. She'll learn lessons she wouldn't learn in school. Shelties are bred to herd. This little toonie might come in handy with our Angus, and maybe even with Jessie.* Allister chuckled at the thought.

chapter twenty-five

An Unfair Accusation and Two Wishes

Allister turned in the front seat of Will's wagon to wave at Mother and Jessie as they stood in the farmyard. Allister saw Tawny pull at her leash then turn and lean against her young mistress. *Hope Jessie and Tawny have a good day while the rest of us are gone.*

It was July 1, the Monday following graduation. It was also Dominion Day, a national holiday. Most of the McRuers were headed to Cherry Creek for the day's celebration. Since Will needed to return that evening to attend to his milking job at his neighbour's farm, he was planning to drive home after participating in the activities in town. Riding directly behind Will's wagon were John, Dan, and Father in the family wagon.

"Thanks for coming to our closing program at school, Will." Delighted that his older brother had invited him and Jim to ride along, Allister was caught off guard by the nastiness of Will's next comment.

"Came because I thought I was going to see two brothers graduate. What happened, Jim? Did Aaalliiisss leave you with all the work again?"

Allister felt red-hot anger building inside him. He gripped the edge of the wagon seat until his knuckles were white—to keep himself from leaning across Jim to punch his accuser. But before Allister could open his mouth to defend himself, Jim spoke up.

"You couldn't be more wrong, Will. I spent all my extra time on things other than studying. Allister tried to warn me, but I refused to listen. Instead, I helped Dan and worked with John's new team of horses. On the weekend before our exams, I finally got down to business. Allister did his best to show me what to study and did double chores without me even asking. Definitely wasn't his fault I didn't do well on my exams! Oh well, it doesn't matter. I don't need any more boring schoolwork! I'm like Dan. My favourite kind of school will always be training the next horse. Speaking of horses, how's Maggie's colt doing? Got him broke to harness yet?"

While his brothers talked, Allister sat silently, his disappointment sweeping over him. *I had hoped Will would be proud of me. Why isn't he done with the taunts? Is he ever going to treat me with any amount of respect? What will it take to change his attitude?*

Allister took a deep breath and released his grip on the wagon seat. *Come to think of it, why does Will's opinion of me matter so much?*

This Dominion Day, Father went off with some of the men he had met while building Cherry Creek's stone schoolhouse. Allister spent the day with his brothers. They watched the parade and several baseball games and took advantage of whatever food was available to buy from the vendor booths.

When his brothers decided to join the dance being held at the new stone schoolhouse, Allister couldn't have been happier. *The one time we came to have a picnic with Father, only the stone shell of the building was close to completion. Now I'll have a chance to look inside the finished school.*

Pausing in front of the school, Allister took in the magnificence of the two storey, quarried-stone building with its numerous windows and broad steps that led to a double wide front door. Inside, he saw a long hallway with a polished wood floor. This part of the school's interior was lit only by the light coming from several tall windows at the end of the hall and the limited light coming through the glass windows in each door to the rooms along the hall. Pale green paint on the plaster-on-lathe walls along the spans aided what light did come in.

Drawn by music and the sound of many rhythmic feet, Allister and his brothers entered the one classroom with its door open. After watching the couples for a bit, Allister excused himself to wander the hallways of the school. It took him a while to find what he was looking for.

"This must be it," he said to the window glass he'd pressed his forehead against. His eyes eagerly took in the large classroom with its huge blackboard. His gaze ran along the opposite wall full of tall windows with bookcases under them. There were charts and maps rolled up, a globe, and thick volumes of dictionaries in three languages—English, French, and one Allister didn't know. A large teacher's desk stood between the blackboard and the numerous tall student desks. "This must be the high school room," he said out loud.

One room for three grades, he thought, *must mean ninth, tenth, and eleventh grades are together. Well, that's better than a one-room schoolhouse with all eight grades, but not much. More importantly, will I ever get to go here? After all I went through the last two years, do I really want to?*

Thrusting his hands into his pockets, he turned to walk back down the hallway and almost ran into Dan. "Find what you're looking for?"

"Yes, Cherry Creek's high school classroom."

"The high school classroom! Why are you looking for that? I thought last year was tough enough for you, with all that studying you did! Besides, what farmer needs more schooling than what you already have?"

"Dan, I'm not sure I want to be a farmer."

"What's the matter with being a farmer? Yes, it's hard work, but it's a good life. When the time comes for each of us younger McRuers to marry, you'll have to agree that a farm is a great place to raise a family!"

"Nothing wrong with farming. It's just that I'd rather use more of my brain and less of my brawn!"

Dan shook his head. "Allister, you have graduated."

Allister studied the tips of his boots and muttered, "No thanks to Father. I missed months of Grade 6 to come to Manitoba. Then I ... we missed an entire year because there was no school to go to when we got here. I missed more school for harvests and building projects on Will's claim. Had to do the double duty of planting after full days at school, so that Father and John could work on this school. With all the interruptions, it's a wonder I was able to get this much schooling!"

Dan crossed his arms. "Nonetheless, you have to reckon with the fact that Father views your education as finished. He expects you and Jim to pitch in full days now."

Allister shuffled his feet as he listened. *I know. I wish it weren't true.*

"Will and John are both busy with their own claims. I am too," Dan continued. "Father will need your assistance more than ever. In fact, all of us could really use your help to meet the homestead improvements needed to keep our claims."

Allister frowned. *Has anybody even considered what I might want?*

Dan thrust his hands into his pockets and smiled at Allister. "Give it time. Making a prairie homestead into a successful farm can be a satisfying venture ... at least, I think so. In any case, Will's already headed back to his place, Allister, so John sent me to find you. Let's find Father and go home too."

Not sure Dan's view of farming would work for him, Allister trudged alongside his brother down the hallway. Their footsteps echoed off the walls and floor of the empty building. *What a wonderful school Cherry Creek has now! Don't want to leave. Wish I could stay. Will I ever get to?*

———◆———

During the next couple of months, Allister worked with Jim from sun up to sundown helping their father manage the McRuer farm. Whenever his father could spare them, Allister and Jim assisted Dan and John with the necessary improvements on their claims. Completing each construction project did give Allister a small sense of satisfaction.

But as the summer days wore on, it became clear to Allister that kind of achievement wasn't enough. *I am not like Father. I'm not my brothers. I am a twin, but Jim and I have different interests. He loves horses. I don't.* Allister shuddered as he remembered the antics of Shalazar, his mother's horse.

What I think I would really like is to be a doctor. Manitoba could use more. He thought about Peter McKinnon, the driver who was so badly injured on Allister's first day in Cherry Creek. Unsure if he would ever be able to make his wish a reality, Allister had never dared to voice it to anyone, not even Jim. *Yes,* Allister thought, *I have completed a major step—by graduating from the eighth grade. But if I'm ever to become a doctor, I know that's not enough.*

Wondering how he could reach for his dream, Allister worked beside Jim on their father's and brothers' land while he waited for the green fields of June to turn brown in the fall. Allister smiled. *Like Dan said, I have time to think about what I really want and how I can possibly get there.*

Endnotes

1. Psalm 96:1–3
2. Genesis 1:1
3. Genesis 1:3–4
4. Genesis 1:12
5. Psalm 8:1–2a
6. Matthew 25:14–15

Glossary

Bannock—a type of flat bread

Beau—a boyfriend

Binder (or reaper)—a horse-drawn farm machine that cuts and binds grain crops into sheaves or bundles

Breech Birth—the birth of a baby hind end, instead of head, first. When a calf or infant is turned the wrong way inside its mother, she has a difficult time with the delivery of her young. In some cases, both the mother and her young die.

Broadcaster—a handheld mechanical device that scatters seed when its crank is turned

Cistern—an underground tank or reservoir for holding rainwater that is collected from the roof of a house. The water is then pumped up and used for washing.

Dump Rake—a wheeled, horse-drawn farm machine with a row of curved tines. The operator lowers the tines to turn mown grass for better drying and to gather the drying grass (or hay) into rows so that it can be pitched onto hay racks or wagons.

Elocution—the study of correct pronunciation and clear, public speaking

Graphophone—a wind-up music machine with a large metal bell. It uses cylinders to play the music.

Harrow—a horse or ox-drawn farm implement that has spikes to break up and smooth soil in preparation for planting

Masonry—the skilled work of laying units of stone or brick to make a building

Plymouth Brethren—an evangelical, Protestant, Christian denomination

Quarry—to cut out or dig out stone for building

Scribbler—a bound booklet of lined paper. A student uses it to keep notes or write his or her homework assignments.

Scythe—a long, curved knife with a long handle. Farmers use it to mow grass or cut grain crops.

Settee—a medium-sized sofa with arms and a back

Stone Boat—a low platform of wooden planks nailed across two logs or a wooden box on wooden runners that horses or oxen pull. In the spring, it is used to transport stones out of plowed fields. In winter, it is used as a sleigh.

Stooking—the action of standing several, bound sheaves of drying grain on their butt ends and leaning them against each other

About the Author

Born in Winnipeg of Canadian parents, Patricia Linson spent her early years with her family in several states south of the border. Whenever she visited relatives in Winnipeg during her teen years, Robert A. McRuer, Patricia's grandfather, told stories of his life on a prairie homestead.

With the financial support of her grandfather, Patricia earned a degree in education. After becoming a naturalized citizen of the US, she began a career as an elementary teacher. Decades later and after Patricia retired, she and her husband, Irv, travelled to southwestern Manitoba to see the McRuer farm for themselves before she wrote *Hope for Allis* and the Allister of Turtle Mountain Series.

Patricia lives with her husband, Irv, in Eagan, Minnesota, and keeps her horse, Grace, at a friend's rural stable. Irv and Patricia's daughter, son-in-law, and three of the four grandchildren live on a farm on the prairie of western Minnesota. The oldest grandson graduated from high school in June of 2017 and began his university studies in St. Paul, Minnesota, that September.

Other Books by Patricia E. Linson
The Allister of Turtle Mountain Series includes three books.

In *Book I: A Boy Called Allis*, eleven-year-old Allister McRuer's fears materialize the spring of 1892 when he and his family arrive at Cherry Creek, the town with the train depot closest to their Manitoba homestead claim. The first dread becomes a reality when Allister learns that the town's schoolhouse is too far from their farm for him and his twin brother, Jim, to walk there every day. How will Allister get any more schooling? While in Cherry Creek, Allister and Jim witness a terrible accident. Learning that the only doctor within seventy miles is out of town scares Allister. If someone in his family were to become sick or injured, who could he get to help? And what could make matters worse? Being called "Allis" constantly by his older brother, Will—who delights in taking advantage of Allister's quick temper.

In *Book III: Becoming Bob*, fourteen-year-old Allister's challenge is to overcome his father's objections to more education. Allister's one thread of hope requires waiting for their one-room school to get a teacher with a high school diploma and persuading that teacher to help him study Grade 9. That strand of hope is threatened when a fire spreads from Turtle Mountain towards the McRuer homestead and the schoolhouse. Can Allister and

his family save their home, livestock, and the schoolhouse? If Allister ever gets his wish to attend high school in town, what can he do to ensure that no one calls him by that obnoxious moniker, Allis?